How to Marry a Highlander

By Katharine Ashe

How a Lady Weds a Rogue
How to Be a Proper Lady
When a Scot Loves a Lady
In the Arms of a Marquess
Captured by a Rogue Lord
Swept Away by a Kiss

Coming Soon
I Married the Duke

Available from Avon Impulse
How to Marry a Highlander
A Lady's Wish

How to Marry a Highlander

A Falcon Club Novella

Katharine Ashe

This is a work of fiction. Names, characters, places, and incidents are products of the author's imagination or are used fictitiously and are not to be construed as real. Any resemblance to actual events, locales, organizations, or persons, living or dead, is entirely coincidental.

EPub Edition AUGUST 2013 ISBN: 9780062273932

Print Edition ISBN: 9780062273949

JV 10 9 8 7 6 5

To all ladies who dare to dream big and then chase those dreams.

Chapter One

Miss Teresa Finch-Freeworth lived in unenviable circumstances.

She did not suffer in penury or even teeter upon the edge of it. She was not the poor ward of a cruel or vindictive guardian and she had not been reduced by circumstances to servile status. She was not unutterably plain or painfully shy. She had not lost her fortune to a gold-hunter or her virtue to a rake.

Instead, the lands of Brennon Manor earned her family above two thousand per annum, sufficient to support Mr. Finch-Freeworth's four hunters and a kennel of no fewer than ten hounds, treatments for Mrs. Finch-Freeworth's frequent invented ailments, too many visits to the track for their three sons, and Teresa's ten weeks in London with Aunt Hortensia the previous year. Teresa's parents were neglectful of her and unsympathetic but not unkind. She was reasonably pretty and possessed of a genuine smile. She had a curious mind and despite her tendency to invent outrageous stories that had all the appearance of veracity—or perhaps because of it—she was well liked in Harrows Court Crossing where she had lived her entire life excepting those ten weeks in London. Her father had set aside for her a marriage portion that was enough to recommend her to a respectable suitor. And finally, at two-and-twenty she still maintained her virtue.

Therein—that last bit—the problem lay.

Teresa had dreams of kissing a man. Many dreams. Vivid dreams.

And not only of kissing.

These dreams were encouraged by her amorously adventuresome maid, Annie, who shared with her mistress more details of her adventures than an unwed lady should ever hear.

In London, however, Teresa's dreams had been augmented by the replacement of an anonymous *kissee* with a real man: the Earl of Eads. This had left her remarkably frustrated and not a little despondent. For good reason: Lord Eads had once seen her, stared at her across a ballroom with great intensity and admiration and perhaps even longing that left her breathless, then promptly left London without seeking her acquaintance; he now resided on his estate in Scotland; a lady could not kiss a man from 300 miles away; and she was beginning to forget what he looked like.

The details she did remember of him nevertheless continued to inspire her dreams: very tall, very broad, and very masculine, with long dark hair, intensely feeling blue eyes, a square jaw, and calves the sight of whose musculature had turned her knees to jelly. He was largely unknown to polite society, and Teresa had learned little more during her time in London: He was a widower; he had lived in the East Indies for many years; he spoke like a barbarian (this information was from Aunt Hortensia, who was a ninny and a snob, so Teresa mostly discounted it); he had seven younger half-sisters, all unmarried; and he was penniless.

It isn't to be wondered at that eighteen months later and no closer to kissing a man than she had ever been, a young woman of spirit and grand dreams would find her current situation intolerable.

That was not, unfortunately, the worst of it.

The worst of it now stood on the threshold of Mrs. Biddycock's parlor, hands clasped behind his back, gazing upon the assembled company of morning callers as though he believed that in order to breathe they had been waiting only for him.

The Revered Mr. Waldon—one part shepherd to his flock, one part youngest son of the youngest brother of a baronet, and three parts conceit—was the most eligible bachelor in Harrows Court Crossing, and everybody expected Teresa to marry him. Mr. Waldon himself expected Teresa to marry him, although he had not yet actually offered for her. But it was generally understood and Teresa was meant to anticipate the event with gratitude and joy.

Now Mr. Waldon surveyed the cluster of ladies gathered about Mrs. Biddycock's tea table with a benevolent eye.

"Good day, Mr. Waldon," exclaimed their hostess. "I've received a letter from my dear cousin in London." She held up several pages. Mrs. Biddycock's cousin's letters were the only news of town that came to Harrows Court Crossing other than the London papers to which Teresa's father would not subscribe because he considered nothing but the *Journal of the Hunt* worthwhile reading.

Mr. Waldon gestured with his hand in an exaggeratedly

courtly manner that struck Teresa as incredibly silly for a local vicar to affect, however exalted of pedigree he was.

"Read on, Mrs. Biddycock," he said, "and I shall attend to your cousin's news with all appearance of interest." He finished this statement with an invasive smile at Teresa and seated himself beside her.

She wished she could inch away. He smelled of eau de cologne, which she did not like—at least not on him. But aside from his elevated opinion of himself he was a decent man and she was reasonable enough to admit that she didn't like him because she felt no desire whatsoever to kiss him.

When the Earl of Eads had stared at her across that ballroom in London she'd gotten hot and unsteady inside, and he hadn't even glanced at her bosom. Mr. Waldon looked at her bosom when he thought she wasn't paying attention. Most men did. Her breasts were ample and her vain mother employed a talented seamstress who knew how to cut gowns for Teresa that were both modest and becoming on her figure.

That night at the ball in London had been no exception; she'd worn maidenly white sparkling with tiny beads and fitted to her bosom to great advantage. But the earl had not given her bosom even a flicker of interest. He had stared at her face.

She liked that about him.

Nevertheless, in her dreams she imagined him looking at her breasts. She imagined letting him touch them and she got hot all over again. Raised to modesty and obedience, she was now nearly desperate to break free of the confines of Brennon Manor and Harrows Court Crossing. Her brief sojourn in London had released all the longing inside her. *I am like flame trapped in a fireplace with the chimney flu shut tight and with piles of kindling a stone's throw away,* she had written to her dearest friend, Diantha Yale. *Suffocating and starving, I will surely die.*

She had a flare for fictional prose. But she felt this acutely.

Now Mr. Waldon stole a glance at her bosom when everybody's attention went to Mrs. Biddycock brandishing the pages. It made Teresa feel nauseated.

"'My dearest cousin Fanny,'" Mrs. Biddycock read. "'I needn't tell you that town is simply bustling with society.'"

But I will anyway, Teresa thought.

"'But bustling it is indeed! You will be delighted to hear that the Misses Blevinses have come down from Shrewsbury with their rascally young nephew, Mr. Pritchard, who—'"

Isn't a day under fifty.

"'—has impressed all the ladies of our acquaintance with his—'"

Remarkably strong aroma of compost.

"'—expertise at—'"

"Balancing a ball upon his nose." Teresa's eyelids were heavy and Mr. Waldon's cologne was making her nose itch. She'd fallen asleep far too late the previous night, worrying over her father's latest hint.

The situation had become dire.

At two-and-twenty, he'd said, his daughter was well past the age at which she should be doting upon her mother at home, by which he meant that she should instead be doting upon Mr. Waldon in his home. Mr. Waldon was not fond of hunting. Since neither was Teresa, her father considered them a perfect match.

"Waldon is the perfect match for you," he'd said, which could not be any clearer, really, and proved how poorly he knew his daughter.

Alongside the nausea and desperation, panic had set in. Sleep was nearly impossible of late.

Mrs. Biddycock had ceased reading. The parlor was silent. Teresa snapped her eyes open. Everyone was looking at her.

Apparently, she had spoken aloud.

"Don't you all recall?" she said. "Mr. Pritchard did that trick with the ball on his nose last Christmas when he was a houseguest of Mr. and Mrs. Kirtle." This was complete invention. "He even got down on his knees like a performing seal. It diverted the children to no end."

"Oh," said one of the ladies sitting opposite, "I remember it now."

"Yes, indeed," Teresa warmed to her story. "Little Sarah found it so amusing that she spit orangeat through her nose, and Mrs. Kirtle"—who was not currently present in Mrs. Biddycock's parlor and was therefore safe material—"was obliged to call upon Doctor Leeds who dosed little Sarah with tonic and put her to bed with a ginger biscuit." A tale woven from whole cloth. She was adept at it. Inventing tales was often the only thing that kept her from running stark naked down the high street singing marching songs. Often she scribbled down her stories to relieve her desperation. To protect the innocent she had invented a fictional town, Harpers Crest Cove, and used false names for her very real characters. But she only ever shared the stories with her younger brother, Freddie, who roared with laughter, and her elder brother, Tobias, who'd read them to his battalion mates during the war.

"Oh, dear," Mrs. Biddycock said. "What a shock for poor Mrs. Kirtle."

"Oh yes. It was horrid. And it did not end there. Mr. Pritchard found that he so much liked little Sarah's excessive hilarity that he joined a traveling show and made a fortune in commissions from local doctors. He came to see the error of his ways eventually, of course," she added somberly, "and gave it all up. I believe he is to visit again at Michaelmas."

The ladies gaped then nodded in anticipation of that delight. Mr. Waldon's brow creased.

Mrs. Biddycock began reading anew. The news was mostly about people Teresa had never heard of and she attended with half an ear. Her father's oblique warning commanded her thoughts.

She had no real justification for not marrying Mr. Waldon. And there was no guarantee that another suitor would ever present himself to her in Harrows Court Crossing. She would be forced to content herself with second-hand stories of Annie's escapades with stable hands and farm lads, and she would spend the rest of her life attending to her mother's imagined ailments.

"'. . . Scottish earl,'" Mrs. Biddycock read. "'I vow, Fanny, it will be a miracle if he finds husbands for even one of those half sisters. His Dark and Scandalous past is whispered in drawing rooms throughout town. His sisters are all hoydens and thoroughly unsuitable for polite company. But I shan't write a word more about them!'"

Teresa sat bolt upright. *Scottish earl?*

"'Except to say,'" Mrs. Biddycock continued, "'that my Henrietta will not attend any event at which we might encounter that heathen brood. If those girls should enter a drawing room to call when we are already there, we will depart at once. Do not mistake me, Fanny: If he were an English earl with one or even perhaps two unruly sisters, I would allow Henrietta to make their acquaintance. An earl is not to be sniffed at. But an impoverished Scotsman with seven sisters to wed in a single season is positively scandalous and I shan't have any of it, unless perhaps one of them were to invite my Henrietta to tea.'"

Teresa's mouth was entirely dry. There could not be more than one Scottish earl with seven unwed half sisters. And now he was in London.

It was too wonderful!

"Oh, dear," she said, leaping up. "I seem to have left my kerchief in the shop. I am terribly sorry to dash away like this, Mrs. Biddycock, but I really must retrieve it before it is carried away by a strong gust of wind or perhaps a sudden flood."

Another lady giggled. "Miss Finch-Freeworth, you are always so amusing."

"Isn't she? The dear girl." Mrs. Biddycock smiled approvingly and rustled pages.

Teresa escaped.

Mr. Waldon came after her.

"Miss Finch-Freeworth, your abrupt departure concerns me." He strode alongside her across the high street muddied by the morning's rain. "Your kerchief must be especially dear to you to cause you to hasten so."

"Yes, I am ever so attached to—"

"And here it is, in your pocket all along." His grip on her elbow forced her to halt. He plucked at the corner of the kerchief poking out of her pocket and drew it forth. "You must have mistaken yourself, but I am happy to restore to you peace of mind."

No one else ever chastised her for her fibs. But Mr. Waldon had no humor in him, and thinking of marrying him weighed on her insides as if she had swallowed Robert Smith's anvil.

"Silly me," she said brightly, and detached herself from his grasp. "My head is all aflutter. I will shortly be departing for London, you see, and have so many tasks to do before I leave that my wits are quite scattered."

"London? I had not heard of this."

"Oh, yes. Within the sennight." She had no travel plans. "My dear friend Mrs. Yale has invited me for a visit." Diantha Yale had done no such thing. No doubt she was now with her adoring husband on their estate in Wales, dandling her infant on her knee by day and by night doing as often as possible what one did to make more infants. Mr. and Mrs. Yale were *very* happily married.

"But why do you go to London," Mr. Waldon said, "when you have everything you wish here?"

He didn't know anything of her wishes. But his face looked a bit like his bleached cravat now and it gave her pause. She placed her hand on his arm.

"Are you unwell, sir?"

He frowned at her hand. "I am well enough," he said stiffly. "I only wonder that you would be comfortable leaving your mother at this time, given her illness."

Fabricated illness. "She is not alone. She has Papa, of course. And Freddie has been sent down from school again."

This time it was for racing chickens in the chancery, which was so wonderfully the truth that she simply could not invent anything better. "He quite dotes on her."

Aha! Freddie had told her at breakfast this morning that their eldest brother, Tobias, had just posted up to London. She would write to both Toby and Diantha, and hope that one of them would be in town. If not, she would force herself upon Aunt Hortensia and steal at least a few days in town before her aunt informed her parents and her father fetched her home.

She started up the street again.

Mr. Waldon kept pace with her. "Allow me to escort you home."

"It is but a mile, and I do know the way." She smiled to ease the sting of rejection. She needn't have. He was constitutionally unable to recognize rejection.

"I have a matter of great importance which I wish to discuss with your father," he said formally.

Dread. More panic. This time speeding through her veins like tiny daggers fashioned of the sorts of shards of ice that one found on windowsills in January.

"You will not find Papa at home, I'm afraid. He went shooting with Freddie this morning." Dear Lord in heaven, *let it be so*.

Mr. Waldon frowned again and fixed her with a challenging regard. "Then I will return later." He extended his hand for her to shake. "Good day, Miss Finch-Freeworth." His palm was smooth and cool, his fingers long and they wrapped around her hand as if they would choke her.

He walked toward the parsonage, his back as rigid as the bell tower. Her stomach twisted in knots.

Mrs. Elijah Waldon.

It simply could not be.

She had an active imagination, but she had few illusions about herself. She was not a noblewoman nor was she stunningly beautiful or an heiress. She was not a fit bride for an earl, even an impoverished earl. But she had the memory of a single, longing gaze and now a great deal of determination and a measure of desperation as well.

She would go to London. She would find him. They would share another longing gaze. *And she would finally have her kiss.*

After that, if she were condemned to spend the remainder of her days in Harrows Court Crossing as the wife of a man she did not like, at least she would have the comfort of knowing she had burned hot and bright for one glorious moment.

Chapter Two

Sunlight peeked through the smudged windowpane, warming the Indian cotton stretched over his shoulders. But Duncan, seventh Earl of Eads, did not move to draw the drapes or open his eyes to appreciate the weather. It mattered nothing to him if the London day shone or fogged or rained. Nor did it concern him if the sounds issuing from the street below his flat were the clatter of hooves and carriage wheels or the shouts of street vendors.

All had fallen away, the present world a vanishing shadow only. With eyes closed, back straight, and legs crossed, he remained still, seeking his center. Deep within, in harmony and acceptance with all the creatures of the universe, peace awaited him. Like the petals of a flower, held close yet ready to spread with the touch of the morning sun, the core of his being—

"Lily! What've ye done wi' ma pink ribbon?"

"I've no touched yer silly ribbon, Effie."

"I'll pull out yer hair if ye've ruined it."

The swish of skirts.

Duncan slowly drew air into his lungs with the power of the muscles in his abdomen.

Slippered footsteps.

"If ye havena got it, then who has?"

"Mebbe ye lost it when ye stopped to flirt wi' those soldiers?"

"I didna flirt." *Giggle.* "I chatted."

In tiny increments, Duncan released the breath, holding steady to his concentration, steady and still and—

"Aye, ye flirted. Deny it if ye will, but I'll no be believing ye."

Another giggle. "There be no harm in flirting, Lily. 'Tis interesting."

"If yer wishing for something interesting, ye might open a wee book once in a while." *Creak of a chair. Flutter of a page turning.* "Both o' ye."

"Then we wouldna need the ribbons, nou, would we, Abigail?" *Laughter.*

Breathe in. Slow, steady, smooth—

"Moira?" *Firm strides between the parlor and bedchamber.* "What did ye do wi' the bill from the fabric shop yesterday?"

"We'd do better to be storing up prayers than dresses to help us all find husbands, Sorcha."

Slow breaths. Seeking serenity. Seeking peace. Breaths as light as feathers yet deep as—

"No one asked ye, Elspeth, so keep yer sermons to yerself."

"Confess, Lily." *Dainty toe tapping.* "Ye hid ma ribbon."

"I didna, I tell ye. Did I, Una?"

"Dinna drag me into yer disputes." *Chuckle.* "I've no got the talent for it."

"Moira, the bill?"

"What're ye reading anyway, Abby?"

"Byron, that immoral—"

"Byron's poetry isna immoral, Elspeth. 'Tis romantic." *Waft of fragrance.* "Here be the bill, Sorcha. I sewed the sleeves this morn."

"Thank ye, Moira."

Breathe.

"Ma pink ribbon!"

"Told ye I didna take it."

Deeper.

"Ye'd best stow it away till ye've guid cause to wear it, Effie." *Firm steps.* "There willna be new ribbons or dresses or anything else—"

"Till a miracle brings us all husbands."

"*Quiet!*"

Duncan's roar echoed through the tiny flat.

Every light feminine footstep went silent. Not a breath stirred except his own, tight and shallow.

Lily giggled. Or perhaps Effie. His youngest sisters, twins, sounded identical to him, even after eighteen months living under the same roof.

But at home in Castle Eads, with plenty of space and too much work, he'd rarely seen his sisters. He'd rarely seen the chilblains on their hands when the hearths were empty and ice clung to the insides of rotted doors. He'd rarely seen the patches in their gowns, the holes in the toes of their shoes, and the dirt beneath their fingernails from laboring as no nobleman's sisters should. And he'd rarely seen their hollow cheeks when dinner was nothing more than mutton broth and barley cakes.

But in this miniscule flat he'd brought them to a fortnight ago, he saw everything: the creases on Sorcha's serious brow, the pallor of Elspeth's sober face, the dampened hope in Moira's lovely eyes, the white knuckles of Lily and Effie's hands holding each other's tight, the avoidance in Abigail's hunched shoulders, and the sympathy in Una's smile.

"Allou a man a moment's peace, will ye?" He unclenched a hand and rubbed the back of his neck.

"Will ye take us to the park today, brither?" Beside Effie, Lily nodded encouragingly. His seventeen-year-old sisters were itching to be out and about.

Elspeth crossed her arms. "So ye can ogle the gentlemen there too?"

"There be no harm in ogling, Elspeth. 'Tis what our brither brought us here to do. Get husbands!"

"There's a wee bit more to getting husbands than ogling, Effie," Una said, a twinkle in her eye. She lifted a commiserating brow at Duncan.

He loved all his half-sisters, but secretly Una was his favorite. With her serene and ready humor she reminded him most of Miranda.

Fortunately, Una wasn't a daft fool who'd thrown herself into the hands of a knave and got herself killed.

"Aye, there's a wee bit more to it," he said. Damn if he knew what. Back home no men of worth came calling on the poor Eads sisters. There were only farm lads, shepherds, and traveling peddlers. And all of his sisters, friendly as their mother had been, welcomed every man into the castle as though he were a saint. Only Sorcha and Una had any idea of the harm that could come to them.

Lily and Effie were hungering for male attention; he could see it in their bright eyes every time a pair of breeches walked by. And Moira was a prize an ignoble man might steal right out from her own home if he found the opportunity—dowry or not.

He couldn't have left them at the castle while he came here in search of suitors. So he'd brought them along in the hopes of finding decent men who'd jump at the chance to marry an earl's sister, however poor.

"I'll take ye to the park, lass," he said.

Effie's brow screwed up. "Dressed like that?"

Behind her open book, Abigail stifled a laugh.

Duncan scowled. He stood and the tunic fell about his thighs. Woven of soft cotton like his trousers, it fit his size far better than anything else he owned.

He moved toward the chamber he'd used as his bedchamber until a fortnight ago. "Outta ma way nou, or I will."

Giggles followed in his wake. He cast back a wink. Then he closed the door and stared at the feminine garments strewn across the bed that four of his sisters shared now.

In his pocket was a total of seventy-two pounds, all the money he had in the world. After the shearing there would be enough to repair the roof on the castle or to eat over the winter. Until then, he had nothing. He didn't know a thing about finding husbands, and the men he knew in London were the sort he would never allow near his sisters. The sort that had taken Miranda.

The land was barren, the flocks decimated from plague the year before, famine before that, and overproduction under his father's haphazard tenure. Whatever stores of grain and good will there'd once been, his father had lost on unwise investments that his second wife had encouraged him to pursue. When Duncan had finally gone home a year and a half ago, after nearly a decade's absence, the place had been in ruin. The bankers had not responded to his pleas. The estate, they said, would never produce. The Eads clan would get no more assistance through honest channels.

There was another option, of course. If he went to Myles and asked for a loan, his former employer would give it to him. But the price Myles would demand for it would be too high. He couldn't do it. That life was behind him. It had to be. For his sisters' sake.

He needed air. Now. And sunlight. Anything to shove away memories of those years in dark alleys and dockyards. Those years when all he'd wanted was to forget the pain.

He tore off the tunic and dressed. A soft knock came at the door. Tying his cravat, he opened it a crack. Una poked her head in.

"Brither, ye've a caller."

He frowned. Few knew the location of his hired rooms in London. "Be ye certain?"

"Aye. And Duncan . . ." Una's blue eyes sparkled. "She's a bonnie young Sassenach."

It would have been remarkable if Teresa had not been quivering in her prettiest slippers. Six pairs of eyes stared at her as though she wore horns atop her hat. She was astounded she had not yet turned and run. Desperation and determination were all well and good when one was sitting in Mrs.

Biddycock's parlor, traveling in one's best friend's commodious carriage, and living in one's best friend's comfortable town house. But standing in a strange flat in an alien part of town anticipating meeting the man one has been dreaming about for eighteen months while being studied intensely by his female relatives did give one pause.

Her cheeks felt like flame, which was dispiriting; when she blushed her hair looked glaringly orange in contrast. And this was not the romantic setting in which she had long imagined they would again encounter each other—another ballroom glittering with candlelight, or a rose-trellised garden path in the moonlight, or even a field of waving heather aglow in sunshine. Instead now she stood in a dingy little flat three stories above what looked suspiciously like a gin house.

But desperate times called for desperate measures. She gripped the rim of her bonnet before her and tried to still her nerves.

The sister that had gone to fetch him reappeared in the doorway and smiled. "Here he is, then, miss."

A heavy tread sounded on the squeaking floorboards. Teresa's breaths fled.

Then he was standing not two yards away, filling the doorway, and . . .

she . . .

was . . .

speechless.

Even if words had occurred to her, she could not have uttered a sound. Both her tongue and wits had gone on holiday to the colonies.

No wonder she had dreamed.

From his square jaw to the massive breadth of his shoulders to his dark hair tied in a queue, he was everything she had ever imagined a man should be. Aside from the neat whiskers skirting his mouth that looked positively barbaric and thrillingly virile, he was exactly as she remembered him. In seeing him now, indeed, she realized that she had not forgotten a single detail of him from that night in the ballroom.

But more than his eyes and muscles and all those other manly bits of him drew her. Much more. The very fibers of her body seemed to *recognize* him, as though she already knew how it felt for him to take her hand. Just as on that night eighteen months ago, now an invisible wind pressed at her back, urging her to move toward him, like a magnet drawn to a metal object. As though they were meant to be touching.

Despite the momentous tumult within her, however, Teresa could see quite clearly in his intensely blue eyes a stark lack of any recognition whatsoever.

Chapter Three

"Weel?" The single word was a booming accusation. "Who be ye, lass, and what do ye be wanting from me?"

It occurred to Teresa at this moment that she could either be thoroughly devastated by this unanticipated scenario and subsequently flee in utter shame, or she could continue as planned.

An image came to her: herself kneeling at the Reverend Elijah Waldon's feet, offering his slippers while he sat in his favorite chair before the fire reading from Butler's collected sermons.

She gripped her bonnet tighter.

"How do you do, my lord? I am Teresa Finch-Freeworth of Brennon Manor at Harrows Court Crossing in Cheshire." She curtseyed upon legs that felt like pork aspic.

His brow creased. "And?"

"And . . ." It was proving difficult to breathe. "I have come here to offer to you my hand in marriage."

Silence.

Complete stillness from the man and seven women staring at her.

A book slipped from a sister's hand and clunked to the floor. "Pardon," the sister mumbled.

"Why, Duncan, ye old trickster," another sister exclaimed. "Ye've gone an found yerself an heiress to surprise us!"

He swung his head to her. "I've no—"

"I'm not an heiress." It was only the second truth Teresa had spoken in a weeklong spree of creative inventions. She'd told her parents that Diantha had invited her to town for a visit. She'd told Diantha and Tobias that she needed new gowns and that Mama had sent her to London on a shopping lark for both of them. And she'd told Annie she was escaping Mr. Waldon, which actually was the truth.

She stepped forward, her heartbeats atrociously uneven. All eyes turned to her, including his, beautiful and so blue—like the most vibrant autumn sky—that it was difficult to think.

"I will have a marriage portion," she said. "But while it is not shabby, it is not by any means a fortune."

"How much is it?" a sister demanded.

"Sorcha!"

"Dinna be missish, Elspeth. If our brither's set to wed her, we should all ken hou much money she'll bring to the family. We've anly got one chance at this." Sorcha's black hair was pinned tight to her head. Of the seven plain gowns in the room, hers was the plainest.

"Well." Teresa bit her lip. "I don't know exactly how much it is. I only know that my mother, who spends far beyond her allowance every quarter, seems satisfied with the amount. So, I—"

He took a step toward her, effectively closing her throat with lock and key.

"I'm no set to wed anybody, Sorcha." He looked directly at Teresa. "As this lass knows." He tilted his head. "Dinna ye, miss?"

He was so large, his shoulders and arms straining at the fabric of his rather shabby coat and the muscles in his thighs defined in trousers that had probably seen too many seasons.

She was staring at his legs. Her gaze snapped up.

Her breath caught somewhere in the region of her ankles. The slightest crease had appeared in his right cheek.

"You are not set to wed me, of course," she managed. "But I hope you will consider it."

A gasp sounded from a sister of no more than seventeen. "Are ye a doxy then, miss?"

"Effie, hold yer tongue," Sorcha said.

"Dinna ye remember? Mither was always going on an on about Father's doxies an hou they always wanted him to keep them like little goodwifies in their own houses an such." Effie brushed a lock of curly hair from her eyes to peer more closely at Teresa. "Mebbe our brither's more like Father than we kent. Are ye our brither's doxy, miss?"

"No!" she exclaimed at the same moment the earl said, "*No.*"

She looked at him hopefully. Hidden within his scowl, a grin seemed to lurk. But she was certainly imagining that. A gentleman would not find such a thing amusing.

"She's a leddy, Effie," the sister who'd dropped the book said.

"Hou do ye ken that, Abigail?" Effie challenged.

"She's no wearing perfume, powder, or baubles," Abigail said with great sense, Teresa thought.

"Una," the earl said, "take yer sisters to the park."

The one that had fetched him, who was about Teresa's age with eyes like her brother's, moved toward the door.

"But I want to stay an see what he says," Effie complained.

"Me too." This one was near enough in appearance to be Effie's twin but smiling with an open friendliness at Teresa.

"Duncan—"

"Go, Sorcha. All o' ye. Go." He waved them toward the door.

"Come on nou. Ye heard our brither." Una lifted a brow at the earl. He shook his head almost imperceptibly and returned his attention to Teresa.

Taking up threadbare cloaks and dart-mended shawls, each sister gave Teresa a curious perusal and headed out the door. Then she was alone with the man she had been dreaming of kissing her and touching her for eighteen months. But now that he stood before her, big and muscular and handsome and studying her intently, he was again abruptly a real man and not only a distant fantasy.

"What do ye have in mind, lass?"

She didn't know what she had expected him to say, but this wasn't it.

"I—" She cleared her throat. "I told you." Her palms were so wet that her bonnet was slipping from her fingers. "I have marriage in mind." And kisses. And touches of the most intimate sort.

He lifted a hand to his chin and his fingertips scratched the whiskers skirting his mouth. "Yer an odd one to be sure, lass."

"I am not a lass. I am a lady."

He swept her figure briefly. She wore her green and ivory pinstriped muslin with the lace collar and tiny sleeves to draw out her mossy eyes and show off her arms. She had even artfully draped a delicate shawl of cream fringe over her elbows. Earlier when she departed Diantha's house claiming she was going to the shops she'd felt perfectly fetching.

Lord Eads did not appear impressed.

"Aye." He nodded. "I'll no doubt yer a gentleman's daughter."

"You needn't doubt anything I say," which was certainly a first for her with anybody and felt very odd indeed. "I am whom I have said and I wish only what I have indicated."

"Anly, hm?" His eyes narrowed. "Lass, a leddy that walks into a stranger's flat an—"

"You are not a stranger. Not—that is—a complete stranger."

He tilted his head.

"You saw me at Lady Beaufetheringstone's ball a year and a half ago." Fire erupted in her cheeks. "You stared at me. And I . . ." She couldn't breathe. "I stared at you."

"Did ye, then?"

"I did. You don't remember it?"

His brow cut down and he searched her face. Her heart pattered.

He shook his head. Her pattering heart plummeted.

He stepped toward her. Up close he towered. Then he did what she'd been dreaming about for months: He touched her. Fingertips beneath her chin, he tilted up her face and his gorgeous eyes studied her. His touch was strong and firm and he smelled of exotic spices that made her feel heady and so good that her eyelids became heavy and her breaths deepened.

"But yer a bonnie thing," he murmured.

"I'm glad you think so. I know this is all rather untoward. But . . . will you marry me?"

"I'll no marry ye, lass. But I thank ye for the offer."

She swallowed, but her throat was still arched and it was a rocky business. "Why not? Do you intend to wed a noblewoman, or perhaps an heiress?"

He released her. "I dinna intend to wed anybody."

"Because you have already been married?"

His brow dipped again but he did not respond.

"I suppose with seven sisters to see wed you've no time for yourself until that is accomplished. Is that the reason you have no plans to wed?"

Now he didn't look amused. "The reason's ma own."

"What if I help you to find husbands for them?" Her mind sped. "If I find husbands here in London for each of them, will you marry me?"

He shook his head. "Yer mad."

"In fact I am quite sane. I am merely proposing to you a wager. I thought gentlemen understood that sort of thing."

A slight smile creased his cheek at the edge of the whiskers. "No that sort o' wager."

"Well if one can wager on carriage races and elections, I don't see why one cannot wager on this too. Will you accept my terms?"

"No."

Teresa's fingers were no longer damp and her heart beat hard. She had come too far and dreamed for too long *and she was too desperate* to easily admit defeat. "What if I found one husband? For one of your sisters?"

Amusement sparkled in his eyes. It made her belly tingle with that wonderful warmth she usually only felt when she was thinking about the stories Annie told her.

"Nou, why would I accept those terms when I wouldna accept better?"

"Hm. Right." She chewed her lip. His gaze slipped down to her mouth. It was the first time he had looked away from her eyes except that perfunctory perusal of her whole person. No man had ever looked at her lips like this, like he was considering them and he liked what he saw. Her breasts, yes. Her lips, never.

Her thoughts got muddled. She could not seem to come up with words.

Ever so slowly his chest rose in a heavy breath, then fell. He did not remove his attention from her mouth.

"Do you want to kiss me?" she whispered.

His gaze trailed up to her eyes. "'Tis a wonder I've no yet thrown ye outta ma house."

"Your so-called house is unfit for an earl and his seven sisters," she said unsteadily. "You will never find respectable husbands for them if you have no place for suitors to come calling."

"Nou ye be insulting ma house an ma hospitality," he said without any rancor whatsoever. "What'll come next from that pretty mouth, I wonder?"

"That I think you really do want to kiss me. And I would very much like you to. You may, you know. Kiss me. Now." She was trembling quite fiercely, but it wasn't to be helped. *She was living her dream.*

He closed the space between them until his broad chest was scant inches from her breasts, and he bent his head. Her eyelids fluttered to half-mast. He would kiss her and her legs were so wobbly she would crumble in a heap at his feet.

"Ye'd best be going nou, Miss Teresa Finch-Freeworth o' Brennon Manor at Harrows Court Crossing in Cheshire."

Good gracious, he'd been paying attention. He said her name with such lush Highland music that the wobbliness spread from her knees to every one of her joints. "I haven't done anything like this before," she said. "But it's you."

"Aye?"

"And I think . . . I know . . . That is . . ."

His whiskers were dark and scant and framed the most perfect lips she had ever seen.

"What have ye heard o' me, lass?"

"Nothing." *Not true.*

"Do ye ken I've no money? That the coffers be dry? Ye'd get nothing from me were I to take ye on, no even a solid roof over yer head."

"I don't know what you mean by 'taking me on.'"

"Ye've run away from home?"

"No. That is, not precisely. I came here to—" She stepped back from him. "You think I have run away from home to become an actress or some other sort of low female and am throwing myself upon you in the hopes that you will become my protector. Like your sister, Effie, said. Don't you?"

He lifted a single expressive brow.

"I am not," she said. "I have the most respectable of intentions toward you. And myself."

"I dinna suppose yer father knows o' this."

"My parents do not know I am here. Naturally," she added. "They would think this as preposterous as you clearly do."

"Mebbe because it is." Then he touched her again, but this time not on her face. He skimmed his knuckles across her shoulder and followed the action with his gaze. A perfectly delicious little shiver wiggled through her.

"What are you doing?" she whispered.

"Lass, do ye ken what a man thinks when a leddy visits him at his home?"

That she was yearning for more touches like that one? "You mean the home he shares with his seven sisters?"

A glimmer lit his eyes. "Touché."

"My lord, I have a proposal for you."

"Anither?"

"Amended, since you rejected my first proposal."

"That I did."

"If I promised that I would not consider myself compromised and demand marriage, would you kiss me now?"

His brow grew dark. "No."

No? What sort of man would not kiss a woman who offered kisses freely?

"Are you rejecting me because you find me unappealing?"

Slowly that single brow lifted again and he tilted his head slightly as though to suggest she was only now beginning to speak foolishly. And his gaze dipped to her mouth anew.

Her stomach did twirling tumbles.

"What if I find a husband for one of your sisters? Would you kiss me in return for that?"

"Ma family's business is none o' yours to meddle in, miss."

"That is no doubt true. But what if in the course of regular social engagements I happened to introduce a suitable gentleman to one of your sisters and she subsequently became betrothed? Then I would not precisely be meddling, would I?"

He scanned her upturned face. "Yer mad as a hatter."

"Not really." Only desperate and somewhat infatuated. "Would you?"

A rumble of laughter sounded deep in his chest. "Aye."

"You agree to it?"

"I've just said so."

She should immediately dash away and begin planning. Diantha and her husband knew plenty of men in town, some of them noblemen. It could not be too difficult to find one who would take an interest in the sister of a Scottish earl, even a poor one. At least three of the Eads ladies were pretty, and one was stunning.

"All right then." She turned toward the door then paused. "What if I find husbands for three of them?" An advantage not pressed was an advantage lost forever. "Would you marry me then?"

"No."

"I could do it." She could? *She would.*

"Ye willna."

"How do you know that? I have an extensive acquaintance in town, among them any number of marriageable gentlemen your sisters could like." A slight exaggeration, soon to be remedied.

But he knew she was speaking with bravado. Skepticism lit his eyes. He crossed his arms loosely. "Do ye, then?"

"I might very well find husbands for three of your sisters. They are lovely, after all."

"They may be." He nodded. "But I'll no marry ye."

"All right. I understand," she said evenly, but her cheeks burned. Her hair must look ridiculous. "But what if I do find husbands for three of your sisters? What would you do?"

"Anither kiss?" His mouth tilted up at one side. It almost seemed like he was enjoying himself.

"That would not be fair, of course." The heat spread from her cheeks to her throat and beneath the lace edging of her bodice. "I should expect something else, something . . . *more substantial* as my prize."

He waited.

"Would you touch me somewhere inappropriate for an unmarried lady to be touched by a man?" she said in a rush.

He simply stared at her.

"Without any promise of marriage," she added quickly. She *was* mad. She would ruin herself with this. But she had already ruined herself. If anyone in society discovered that she had pursued an interview with a bachelor in his rooms she would be cut from every respectable house in town.

"This wee wager is getting interesting," he murmured, and his voice sounded somehow deeper. It sent a delicious little thrill of sensation right up the center of her belly.

"I'm not planning to set myself up as anybody's mistress," she clarified. "It's only that . . ." She straightened her shoulders. "Well, it's really none of your business, especially if you won't marry me."

"I'll agree to it."

Her breaths hitched. "You will?"

He nodded slowly. "Aye."

Her throat got caught on several swift swallows. "All right." Press the advantage. "What about five?"

"Five touches?" His eyes glimmered with something new, something hot and intentional.

"Five husbands," she said thickly. "For your sisters. What if I find husbands for five of your sisters?"

"Ye willna."

"I might."

"Unlikely."

"But not impossible."

"Nearly."

"Do you have such a poor opinion of your own siblings?"

"One or two."

She shook her head. "Now you are telling untruths. You care for them all. I can see it in your eyes."

"That daena mean I think they'll find husbands easily."

"They won't have to. I will. So, what about five?"

"What terms be ye offering, lass?"

"If I find five husbands, you must make love to me."

She'd said it! Just like that. And her pulse was careening and he was looking at her like a madwoman, which was a perfectly reasonable conclusion for him to come to. But the half smile still shaped his gorgeous mouth.

"Saucy lass."

"If that is the worst you can say after I have offered such terms, then I begin to doubt your morals, my lord."

"I have no morals, Miss Finch-Freeworth. Didna ye learn that in yer research o' me?"

In the past three days of visiting acquaintances about London, when she had inquired of Lord Eads everybody always wanted to gossip about his unsavory past, his years in the East Indies and, more recently, years during which it was thought he'd been in London but no one in society ever saw him. Only yesterday Diantha had said in no uncertain terms that Lord Eads was not a man to be pursued. She refused to explain, but Teresa had rarely seen her good-natured friend so alarmed. "I . . . Someone might have mentioned it."

"An ye didna listen?" He shook his head. "No as clever as I'd been thinking ye, after all."

Her heart did a little skip. "You think me clever?"

His eyes glimmered.

"Clever enough to find husbands for five of your sisters?"

He shook his head.

"So then if you don't believe I will, why won't you agree to my terms?"

He looked quite directly into her eyes. "I didna say I wouldna, did I?"

Her entire body flushed with agitated heat. "You will?"

"Ye drive a hard bargain."

He was laughing at her now. But she was, after all, laughable at this point. She smiled though she suspected she should not.

"Then it seems we have a deal," she said. "But . . ."

"But?"

"What if I manage to find seven husbands?"

"Lass—"

"What if I do?"

His gaze hooded. "Name yer terms."

"Will you marry me then?"

"Why would I marry a woman I dinna know from Eve who's given away her virtue to a man in a wager?"

"Not to *any* man. To y—" She bit her lip. "Oh. You are teasing me, aren't you?"

"I may be."

"I like it."

"Dinna become accustomed to it."

"Why? Won't you tease me again?"

"Aye. But ye havena asked *ma* terms."

"Oh! I didn't think. I'm not in the habit of making wagers, you see."

"Ye dinna say?"

"What are your terms, my lord?"

"Ye've a month or the wager's a forfeit."

"A *month*? But I cannot possibly—"

"Those be ma terms, lass. Accept or withdraw."

She pulled in a breath of courage. "I accept." She thrust out her hand. "Shall we shake on it?"

It was perhaps a mistake to seal the agreement in this manner. His hand was large and strong and encompassed hers entirely and made her feel tiny and entirely in his power. Perhaps the gossips weren't spreading empty rumor. Perhaps he was a dangerous man and that longing gaze they had shared at the ball had been more dream than reality. A tremor of fear slithered through her.

She forced her gaze up and glimpsed in his eyes the oddest hesitation. It looked almost like the fear she was feeling.

"My lord," she breathed. "I think perhaps—"

The door snapped open. "Duncan!"

Their hands flew apart. They both stepped back.

Effie halted, eyes wide.

Her twin skipped in behind her. "Abigail finished her book. She wants to go to the shop and trade it in for anither."

Sorcha came through the door removing her mended gloves. She stopped and they all stared at Teresa.

"I should be going now." She curtseyed. "My lord. My ladies." She went past them and through the door and down the steps, heart in her throat and—for the first time since that night at the ball—an unsettling sensation of utter confusion spreading through her.

Sorcha turned to him. "What did she really want, Duncan? Money? I suppose ye put her to right aboot that."

Duncan stared out the open door through which his sisters were entering and through which *she*—the woman who had inspired his flight from London eighteen months earlier—had departed.

"Tell yer sisters to pack their bags," he heard himself say. "We're moving."

Chapter Four

How on earth would she secure even one husband for seven impoverished ladies when she could not secure one for herself?

Teresa rested her chin on her palm and stared out the window onto the street before Diantha's townhouse. According to the footman, Mr. Yale would be home shortly. Diantha would tell her nothing of Lord Eads, but Teresa understood that her husband knew the earl quite well.

As she watched carriages clatter by on the street she catalogued the sisters. One of the two whose name she did not yet know was clearly the beauty of the family, followed by the vivacious twins, Effie and the other. Abigail was pretty too, and sensible; she'd known Teresa was not a doxy. Una had a clever eye and ready smile. Sorcha was all business. Judgmental, prim, and self-possessed, Elspeth reminded her of Mr. Waldon.

She had plenty to work with, but it was probably best to begin with the quality that men noticed immediately in a woman: beauty. It stood to reason that if she found a husband for the beautiful sister first, the rest would soon become known to his friends and acquaintances.

A horseman dismounted before the house. He wasn't Mr. Yale, but as the only man in the world that thought highly of her, her brother Tobias was always welcome company.

She met him at the door. "Have come to see Wyn? He mentioned that you were to call on him."

"He knows a few fellows that might help me get a leg up at the War Office." His handsome face glowed with pleasure. "But that's not my purpose today. I've come to escort you shopping."

"Shopping?"

His brow lifted beneath hair two shades darker than hers. "Is it me or shopping that inspires this listlessness?"

"Shopping, of course. I know. Unprecedented. Toby . . . I . . ."

"What is it, T? You look pretty as a picture today, but all the same, glum. Not like you at all."

She had not told Diantha. She had not told Annie. The only people that knew were the earl and his sisters, and she was perfectly at sea. She was coming to see that if one wished to achieve grand dreams, one needed help from trusted friends.

"Yesterday afternoon after three days of research among the gossips of London, I discovered the address of the Earl of Eads and paid him a call. He is a penniless Scotsman with an unproductive estate and seven half sisters to wed off, and I made a wager with him that if I found them all husbands within a month he must marry me."

Her brother stared at her quite the way the earl and his sisters had the day before.

"Are you insane?"

She slumped down in a chair. "That's what he said."

"Sounds like a sensible fellow."

"I am *not* insane. I do not wish to marry Mr. Waldon but Papa is determined, and I—"

"You think your only option to Waldon is *this?*"

"I cannot bear the idea of it, Toby! Merely sitting beside him makes me feel all prickly and ill. He's not really that awful. It's only that I am terrified of spending the remainder of my life as his chattel."

"Well, I understand your hesitation there. Waldon's a thorough prig. But you needn't throw yourself on the mercy of an unknown Scot to find a husband. Diantha must know plenty of gentlemen who'd be glad to court you."

"She and Wyn have taken me about town. But, you see, I made the acquaintance of Lord Eads when I was in town with Aunt Hortensia. Rather, not quite his acquaintance . . . But . . ." She folded her hands. "I want him."

"You want him?" His eyes widened. "Oh, no, T. Don't tell me that when you were here last year you—"

"I didn't do anything."

"Because I've heard stories from the grooms in Father's stables. I know that maid of yours is—"

"I didn't do anything! I only saw him and, well, something about him . . . fits. Toby, please try to understand."

"But this is—"

"I know!" She leaped up. "It's madness. I have no idea why I feel so strongly about a man about whom I know next to nothing. But I know scads and scads about Mr. Waldon and I simply abhor him."

Her brother's brow crunched. "Those don't follow."

"Of course not. But I've done it, Toby. I've made the wager with Lord Eads despite his considerable reluctance. He doesn't believe I will manage it."

"What exactly did he say when you made this offer?"

"He said he would not do it." She suspected he had finally agreed only to make her go away. "If a lady asked you to marry her, would you?"

"If she'd called in secret at my home and wagered herself against my sister's future? No."

"Why not? I am not an antidote and I do have a marriage portion."

"T, if a man's got any honor in him he wouldn't treat a lady in a manner he wouldn't want his own sisters to be treated, would he?"

He had a point. And Toby didn't know the half of it.

She didn't care what the gossips said about the earl's unsavory past. He was trying to protect her from herself.

"Listen here, T, I won't let you go near him again until I've spoken with him and learned something of his character and his intentions toward you," Tobias said firmly.

"He doesn't have any intentions toward me. I think he would rather I go away."

"Be that as it may, he's got fodder for gossip now that could ruin your reputation."

"Toby, Papa and Mama have determined that Mr. Waldon is my destiny. If I ruin my reputation here perhaps he will refuse to take me."

"And every other man!"

She shrugged. "Then it seems that my brothers' future wives will be obliged to put up with old spinster Aunt Teresa as a permanent house guest."

He chuckled. "Nonsense. Now come on. Collect your cloak and we'll find some gowns and what-have-you's so Mama will be happy you've done your duty to her."

She pursed her lips and shifted her eyes away.

Her brother's mouth flattened. "You invented that story, didn't you?"

"I did. I came to London only to find Lord Eads and make him marry me."

"An I for one think it a grand plan." The voice that came from the doorway was clear and warm.

"Lady Una Eads and Lady Moira Eads," the footman announced.

Aha! *Moira* was the beautiful one.

Teresa went forward. "How kind of you to call. I never imagined you would."

Una's vibrant blue eyes met hers honestly. "We almost didna. Ye left no card. We were at a loss until I demanded that ma brither reveal how ye kent o' him. He refused to tell me more than the name o' the gentleman whose house this is."

Teresa's heart did a little twist. He had not told her the truth. He did remember seeing her that night with Diantha at Lady Beaufetheringstone's ball.

She recalled her manners. "Mr. and Mrs. Yale are not in now. But please allow me to make you acquainted with my brother."

Tobias bowed. Una nodded. Moira performed a lovely

curtsey, her satiny dark curls dangling about her brow and neck and her gentle blue eyes downcast.

"Miss Finch-Freeworth," Lady Una said, "our brither wouldna explain yer extraordinary proposal, so we've come to make sense o' it."

"There is really nothing to make sense of."

Una's slender brows rose. Tobias folded his hands behind his back.

"I wish to marry him."

"That we already understood," Una said with a slight grin. "But he's flustered enough aboot it that we wanted to hear the rest o' it from ye."

"You flustered an earl, T?" Tobias said. "Well done."

"I'd the same thought maself, sir." Una's grin widened.

Tobias smiled back at her. He seemed completely unaffected by the Aphrodite beside her.

Teresa's pulse was spinning. *She had flustered him.* "I made a wager with him that if I found husbands for you and your sisters he must marry me."

"He told me as much, though I thought he was funning." Una's eyes sparkled with amusement. "In truth it seems a fine plan. But are ye a virtuous leddy, Miss Finch-Freeworth?"

"Now see here, miss," Tobias said, his shoulders squaring. Lady Una set a curious gaze on him. "That is, my lady," he amended. "My sister is the best sort imaginable. If she wishes your brother to court her then she must know he is an honorable man."

"Aye, he is. A' times too honorable for his own guid."

Moira looked between them, a little smile playing about her rosebud lips.

Una nodded decisively. "Weel, I dinna suppose we're helping ye match-make by holding ye here nou, are we? Ye'd best get on wi' it, Miss Finch-Freeworth." Her eyes sparkled.

Teresa's breath shot out in relief. "Do call me Teresa."

"If we're to be sisters," Moira said sweetly, "ye must call us by our given names too." She extended a delicate hand for Teresa to shake. "I'm Moira, and I hope ye marry our brither, Teresa."

Tobias cleared his throat. "Ladies, with all due respect to my sister's uncanny sense of a man's good character and to your filial loyalty, I insist on meeting Lord Eads before this outrageous program proceeds any further."

"Naturally," Lady Una said.

"And I should like your word," he said, his face becoming very sober now, "that news of this project will remain among us."

"Sir," Lady Moira said softly, "since she's to be our sister, it wouldna serve us otherwise, would it?"

He looked to Lady Una who smiled.

"All right." He stepped forward and took Una's hand on his arm. "Shall we be off?"

The sisters had walked over. Teresa was accustomed to walking miles in the countryside, but not in London.

"We're no living in the flat nou," Una said. "We anly walked ten blocks."

Tobias met Teresa's gaze and he nodded once. Her heart warmed. He would find a carriage for them. She suspected he had plenty of things on which to spend his allowance, especially now that he was currying favor with gentlemen who could help him find a position in the War Office, which was his fervent hope. But he would help the poor Eads sisters because it meant helping his own sister. He was a prince among brothers.

He sent a footman to the corner to hail a hackney cab and they set off. When the carriage drew up on the outside edge of the fashionable quarter of town before a tall, many-windowed building flying the flag of Britain, Teresa's brow wrinkled.

"This is a hotel. It cannot be—"

"Home," Una said. "Aye, 'tis nou."

Neither elegant nor shabby, fashionable or dowdy, the Hotel King Harry was a modest place with rugged, sturdy appointments and equally rugged and sturdy footmen. Una and Moira led them toward a door from which issued forth the uncertain notes of a pianoforte.

The scene within was considerably worse than that which Teresa had witnessed at the earl's flat.

In the center of the parlor young Effie, giggling raucously, twirled about between two grinning soldiers in grimy uniforms. Her twin sat at the piano, poking out the tune, with Elspeth glowering at her shoulder. In a corner Abigail was curled up in a chair with her feet tucked under her, a book on her knees. A birdlike, grey-haired lady garbed entirely in black lace and wool sat at a window amidst the sisters, her gaze trained on the street.

"Good gracious," Teresa uttered under her breath.

Una's lips twitched. "Meet ma sisters, Teresa."

Lady Effie twirled around. "Miss Finch-Freeworth! Ye needn't find a husband for me. I already have two suitors." She giggled again and threw her hand into a soldier's.

Her twin's playing faltered. "Oh! She is here!" She stood and knocked the sheet music off the stand with her elbow. "Welcome back, miss."

Lady Elspeth frowned. Lady Abigail's head came up as though she were waking from a deep sleep.

With a decisive breath, Teresa marched into the room. "Good day." She went to the closest soldier. He smelled of ale and something else that was very nasty.

"Well there, miss. Come to join the dancing?" He leered at her bosom. "We'd like that, wouldn't we, Ned?"

Ned smirked.

"Sir," she said bracingly, "I regret to inform you that these ladies are already spoken for by respectable gentlemen who will be calling shortly," she fabricated. "I recommend that you depart before they discover you here."

The soldier gave Tobias an assessing look. "Is this one of them?"

"This is my brother. He is with the War Office and it is his job to detain and interrogate former soldiers who have no gainful employment."

The soldier's eyes narrowed. But he said, "Come on then, Ned. No fun to be had here."

Teresa released a silent breath of relief, never more grateful that her brother was a well-built man. He'd drawn himself up to his full height, and as the soldiers passed him at the door they gave him wide berth.

Una's eyes twinkled. "Are ye with the War Office, sir?" she said when the soldiers had gone.

"I have hopes." His smiled and Teresa's heart swelled with affection.

Effie's twin came forward. "I'm Lily. Have ye truly found husbands for us all?" Her eyes were nearly as pretty as Moira's, and considerably more candid.

"No."

Effie's mouth set in a pout. "Then why did ye send those lovely gentlemen away?"

"Because they were not in fact lovely or gentlemen." Teresa looked about at the seven people staring at her. The old woman in black had not removed her attention from the street. "If we are to do this successfully, we must do it right, which means socializing only with men suitable to court an earl's sister."

"But—"

"Listen to the lass, Effie," the earl said in his deep, delicious rumble behind her. "She's got yer best interests in mind."

Teresa turned to him and was glad there were eight other people in the room or she might have done something astoundingly forward. He looked as rough and barbaric and thrillingly virile as the day before, and she was convinced that the devil himself had created the Earl of Eads to make her think wanton thoughts.

"Havena ye, lass?" he said.

"Yes. As well as my interests. But I would prefer it if you did not call me lass."

"Would ye?"

"I would as well," Tobias said firmly and moved beside her.

Lord Eads frowned. "Suitor?"

"No, Duncan." Una grinned. "This is Mr. Finch-Freeworth. Teresa's brither."

The earl's shoulders seemed to relax. He nodded at Tobias. "Come to chaperone?"

"I have."

"Which won't be necessary at present," Teresa said, "as our business today is entirely of the feminine sort. But you are certainly welcome to come along if you wish, Toby." She forced her attention away from the earl and studied his sisters gathered around. Their gowns were threadbare and their slippers scuffed. That could be easily remedied; between her and Diantha's wardrobes they would find gowns and whatnot to suit. "We must return to my lodgings and . . ." She could not say what she intended. She could not shame him like that. "Make some plans," she finished. "On this occasion I should like to take Ladies Moira, Lily, Abigail, and Una." They were the prettiest, excepting defiant Effie. "May I, my lord?"

He nodded. "Ye heard the leddy," he said to his sisters. "Be aff wi' ye."

Elspeth's nostrils looked pinched. "I will remain here and read to my sister from my latest treatise on the proper comportment of modest females."

Effie's brow was dark. "I dinna think I like ye, Miss Finch-Freeworth. Ye remind me o' our old nurse."

"That'll do, Effie." The earl's voice was a warning growl.

Teresa went forward and looked Effie directly in the eye. "Do not fret. I have great plans for you, Lady Effie." Making certain she didn't lose her innocence to a two-penny ex-soldier, for instance. She lowered her voice. "But now I need you to arrange Lady Elspeth's hair in a fashion that will not frighten off crows. Will you do that for me?"

Effie wiggled her brows. "I may like ye after all." She pulled Elspeth out the door.

"The carriage awaits, ladies," Tobias said.

Lily went out with a light step, Moira following. Abigail trailed reluctantly behind. Teresa bit her lip. Perhaps the bookish sister shouldn't be thrown into socializing immediately.

"She willna be alone, Teresa," Una said. "We'll be wi' her."

"How did you know what I was thinking?"

"Because I've the same worry."

Teresa took Una's hand. "I think I will be fortunate to have you as a friend."

Una's eyes crinkled at the sides. "Yer the first English leddy who's spoken kindly to us since we've been in London. I'm already the fortunate one."

"My lord," Tobias said, "I will return momentarily."

Lord Eads nodded. Tobias offered his arm to Una and went out.

"Your sisters gave you away, you know," Teresa said, turning to the earl. "If you were trying to escape me by moving across town, you clearly do not know how much gossip is being bandied about concerning you and your sisters. I heard about this"—she gestured to the hotel—"before breakfast." Invention. But it was best to show a powerful offense.

"Blast it, woman. Ye said to move outta the flat, so I moved them."

He had followed her advice. "I meant into a house, of course."

"Managing female."

"We made a deal, my lord."

"I'm weel aware o' that."

"Why didn't you send me a note telling me of your new direction?"

"Do ye be wanting a man to be sending ye private messages at yer friend's house nou?"

"You could have disguised it as a posy."

"I'm no courting ye, Miss Finch-Freeworth."

True. It was rather the opposite. She could not deny that she liked the feeling of power it gave her to command a great big titled nobleman to do as she wished. At home her parents never paid her wishes any heed. But her dreams of being swept off her feet by a man had involved him doing the sweeping, not her.

That was childish, she supposed. This was real. Her future depended upon it.

"I will accomplish what I have promised." She said it as much to convince herself as him.

"We'll see."

"Why did you say you did not remember seeing me at that ball last year when in fact you did?"

He said nothing for a moment, then: "Guidday, miss." He bowed.

"Good day, my lord."

She left. She had a month. Twenty-nine days now, to be precise. It wouldn't do to badger him unnecessarily. Even Tobias, a gem of a man, didn't like badgering. She had plenty of time to come to understand the man she was courting, and perhaps even to secure husbands for one or two of his sisters before someone in society discovered her program and she was cut from every drawing room in London.

Now, however, she had no time for pessimistic musings. She must outfit a bevy of bonnie lasses.

Duncan watched her brother hand her into the cab. As she stepped up, her cloak tugged tight against her full, round behind and Duncan's cravat felt two sizes too tight.

He should not be allowing this. Two days earlier he should have told her to leave him be in no uncertain terms, then he should have said nothing to Una. But he'd been a bit outta his mind at the time.

She had come *to him*.

It wasn't to be believed. He'd thought about her often in the past eighteen months while he'd been trying to make something of the disaster his father left of the estate. He'd not been able to forget her. Only twice in his life had the mere sight of a woman across a room spun his world upside down.

The first time that happened, his fragile Marie paid for it with her life and the life of their wee bairn. The doctor said it'd been the babe's size—big like his father—too big for his dainty mother to bring forth. Even seven years later, the dark hollowness that had grown inside him from the day he'd held her breathless body in his arms and knew he'd killed her still clung to him. He'd not curse another woman like that. Miss Teresa Finch-Freeworth with her outrageous propositions and warm, vibrant smile deserved better.

He scowled. He'd enough of managing females now, anyway. Seven of them.

Seven husbands for seven brides . . .

She meant to go through with it. If she did, he'd be honor bound to kiss her, touch her, and make love to her. Then to wed her.

He couldn't allow it. He'd not use a woman like that for

any reason, not when he didn't intend to marry her. But she was as determined as she was bonnie. He'd have to deter her from pursuing her program.

Finch-Freeworth closed the carriage door and with a firm stride returned to him.

"My lord, your sisters seem like gentlewomen and I don't mind my sister going about town with them. But I'll know what intentions you have toward her or I'll make an end to their acquaintance this instant."

Duncan liked his directness. "I've no intentions toward yer sister."

"She said that. But she's prepared to go to a great deal of trouble on your behalf. If she succeeds—"

"She willna." He'd make certain of it. He knew a few places in town where bachelors were in short supply. He'd fill the month with visits to every one of them.

"Probably, but she's a good-hearted girl and I won't stand for her being hurt. Or worse." He stood in a fighting stance now. Clearly he had soldiering in his past. "Are you a man of good character where women are concerned?"

"If ye care to learn o' ma character, sir, ye'd best be inquiring o' Yale. He'll tell ye all ye need."

There. He'd done it. Wyn Yale—damn his hide—would tell Finch-Freeworth the truth, and they'd cut the connection. Then the temptation to proceed with her as he'd done the last time a woman's smile made his heart stop would be gone.

"I'll do that." With a bow, Finch-Freeworth departed.

Sorcha appeared beside Duncan. "Who was that?"

"Her brither."

"Hm. She's resolved, then."

"Aye."

"No as resolved as I am to make something o' that blast south burn. Duncan, ye've got to allou me to draw funds from the bank to—"

"No."

"Why not?"

"Because there no be funds in the bank to be drawn."

"There must be. Yer hiring four chambers in this hotel an breakfast, lunch, tea, an dinner every day."

"I've no paid a penny for those." He'd called in an old debt from the hotelier, a man for whom he'd done several jobs the likes of which his sisters would never imagine.

"But, what—"

"Dinna ask, Sorcha." He set a hard gaze on her. "I've told ye afore: Ye dinna want to ken."

She nodded briskly, but her brow was tight. Along with Una she was the best of the lot. While he'd worked for Myles here in town to earn money to send home, for five years she'd kept the estate running with that money. Her competence in managing the land was all that had stood between his people and starvation.

"I've so many ideas, Duncan, but I need capital to pay for them. I'm that frustrated. If I could make a wee improvement here or there, I could do so much." She was silent a moment. "Ye've got to wed an heiress. 'Tis the anly way."

He stared out the open door. "I canna."

"Stubborn ox. Too guid for a rich tradesman's daughter?"

He allowed himself a smile he did not feel. "Aye. Something like that."

She let that sit for a moment. Then: "Yer lying to me. Una told me the truth o' it."

Una was too perceptive. She understood why he refused to wed again.

"Sorcha, ye've got to marry."

"Duncan—"

"I'll no hear otherwise. Chuise a man. Any man that can give ye a bairn. A widower, if ye wish: a man that's already proved he can father sons. Bring him afore me an I'll see it done to yer liking." By ancient right the Eads earldom allowed a woman to inherit and pass the title to her child. No lord of Eads had ever failed to produce heirs, but there was a first for everything.

Beneath the cap of smooth black hair tied tight at the nape of her neck, Sorcha's eyes flashed like a brewing storm. "Ye'll have to tie me up an drag me to the altar." There was no childish defiance in her face, only cool, clean determination—the other side of the coin from the vibrant, fiery-haired woman who'd stood before him quivering yet insisting he wed her.

"Yer too much like I was, sister," he said. "Ye'll be worse aff for it in the end."

She hitched a fist on a hip and cocked her head. "Tell me, brither: Hou would it be possible to be worse aff than ye nou?" She strode up the stairs.

Duncan drew his watch from his pocket. Thick gold with the crest of clan Eads embossed upon it, it was the last family heirloom remaining. It'd have to go now. He'd seen the quick calculation in the lady's lily pad eyes; he couldn't have her spending her pin money on his sisters. That, and if he was going to distract the matchmaker from her program he'd need to look the part of a gentleman. A trip to the pawn broker then to the tailor, and he'd be ready to embark on his own mission to save the virtue of a clever maiden from himself.

Chapter Five

There were lessons to be learned from taking four Highland Scotswomen of modest means and little London experience to the drawing room of one of society's grandest ladies at the fashionable hour.

For instance, nine out of ten London ladies and seven out of ten London gentlemen do not apparently understand brogue. Also, three out of five debutantes are atrociously spiteful, and two out of five young gentlemen actually emit drool from their mouths when introduced to a girl of Moira's beauty. Finally, Scottish ladies do not hold their tongues when their elders chastise them unjustly.

The visit to Lady Beaufetheringstone's house was not, however, a thorough wash. Tobias's championing of the Eads ladies was enough to make a sister cry in gratitude. Lady B was splendid too. Upon their departure she apologized for the horrendous manners of several of her guests ("I will cut them from my guest list!") and said she wished Lady Una and Lady Moira to attend her ball three days hence. Young Lady Lily may attend too if she could restrain herself from knocking over every potted plant, vase, and footman. Lady Abigail was welcome to enjoy the Beaufetheringstone library to her heart's content during the ball ("Really, my dear, dancing is the least of what goes on at one of my balls. But you may bury your nose in a book if you prefer.").

All in all, it could have gone worse.

Teresa sank back against the squabs of the carriage Toby had hired for them and closed her eyes.

"I'm sorry it didna go aff as ye planned," Una said. "I'm afeart we havena much talent for high society."

"Yet." Teresa sat straight up. "You only require a touch of town bronze, which will come in time." Time she did not have. Twenty-six days and counting. "Isn't that true, Toby?"

He smiled comfortably at Una. "Quite right."

Una returned his smile.

"May we stop at the bookshop on our way home?" Abigail asked.

Teresa needed a nap then a pot of tea before she started planning again. And she was eager to take up her pen and add the knocking-over-the-footman incident to her latest little tale about the make-believe town of Harpers Crest Cove. Freddie would love it.

But Moira's face was drawn and Lily was tucked miserably into her corner of the carriage, entirely unlike her usual sunny self.

"Yes. Let's stop at the bookshop," Teresa said. "If I remember correctly, there is a shop nearby that sells the tastiest lemon ices imaginable."

Lily's eyes brightened. "I do like ices."

"Ye like all confections," Abigail said. "Ye even liked that book about confections I found for ye last week."

Lily smiled, restored to her usual glow. "I should have liked to read it through, but I'd nothing to trade for it."

"Ah." Tobias reached into his pocket. "It just so happens that I have a book here that I've been meaning to sell." He pulled forth a small volume. "We shall trade this for your confectioner's book, Lady Lily."

"Oh, thank ye!" She took the proffered volume cheerily.

Una caught Teresa's eye and her brow lifted. Teresa offered a breezy smile, but she'd glimpsed the title. It was her brother's most cherished book, a history by an ancient Greek historian that he had carried with him to war and back again.

"Thank ye, sir," Una said. "Yer kind to our family."

"I pray you, don't thank me, my lady," he replied. "It's my pleasure."

The bookshop was an elegant little cabinet at the end of a long corridor from an unremarkable door leading off the street, snug, smelling of lemon polish, and ceiling to floor with books. But the wood of the bookshelves sparkled, the chairs arranged here and there were beautifully upholstered, and several very fine albeit tiny oil paintings decorated the miniscule wall space. The shopkeeper greeted them distractedly. Then abruptly he came to attention and slid off his stool behind the desk. He straightened his spectacles and smoothed out his otherwise neat waistcoat.

"Good day, ladies." He bowed. "Lady Abigail," he said in a quieter voice. She gave him a little smile and a nod then went to a shelf and pulled down a book.

"Is this the one ye showed me afore, sir?" she said.

"Yes." He hurried to her. "Yes. That's the one."

Una, Moira, and Lily wandered deeper into the shop. Teresa took her brother's arm to detain him.

"You went off so swiftly yesterday after our ride in the park that I hadn't the opportunity to speak with you privately," she whispered.

"Ah, yes. Sorry about that." He seemed distracted.

"And . . .?"

"And?"

"It's been three days and you haven't said a word about your conversation with Lord Eads. Did you speak with him?" The earl had not accepted the invitation to walk in the park with his sisters the previous day, and the day before that had been taken up entirely with measuring and hemming gowns. Teresa was rather desperate to see him again. But she supposed he saw no reason for that unless he owed her payment on their wager.

Abigail and the shopkeeper stood with their heads bent close, whispering earnestly. He gestured with the book as though to emphasize a point. She laughed. Abigail—serious, bookish, quiet Abigail who had not spoken a single syllable at Lady B's drawing room—*laughed aloud*. It sounded like rusty bells tinkling. But the shopkeeper smiled as though he'd won a prize.

Teresa stared. Then, as the shopkeeper moved half a step closer to Abigail, her belly filled with butterflies.

"Toby?" she whispered. "Did Lord Eads meet with your approval? I must assume he did or you would not be ferrying his sisters about in a carriage you hired."

"I didn't hire it. Eads did, of course." Tobias was still facing her but his gaze was fixed deeper into the shop. Teresa didn't have to follow his attention to know where it rested.

Her nerves sang. Abigail and the bookseller! *And Lily and Tobias?* Teresa hadn't seen any sign of her brother's especial interest in that twin as yet. But he had given away his most cherished keepsake for her. Could it be love already? It must at least be strong admiration.

She drew in a steadying breath. She mustn't get ahead of herself. But now Abigail was looking straight into the shop-keeper's face and her hand rested beside his on the open page.

"Tell me, Toby." Nerves cracked her voice.

Tobias's attention came back to her a little dazedly. She resisted turning to see if Lily's eyes were likewise hazy.

"I spoke with Yale," he said. "He admitted that Eads has an unsavory past, but before that there was a tragedy in the family." He looked grave. "It seems his full sister perished under peculiar circumstances while he was in the East Indies. It drove his father into the grave. Soon after that, when Yale met Eads in the Indies, the earl was in mourning over the death of his wife—a French girl." Tobias shook his head. "Poor fellow, losing both his sister and wife in so short a time."

"I should say so," she uttered, the butterflies hardening into a lump in her midsection.

"But Yale did make one thing clear, T. The earl is a man of honor. He said he hadn't always liked Eads, but he'd trust him with the welfare of a woman any day."

Teresa's heart thudded very fast. "Does that mean that you will allow the wager?"

Tobias nodded reluctantly. "I'll allow it."

"And you won't tell Papa or Mama?"

"I'd be as insane as you to tell them."

Abigail was all private smiles and soft blushes on the carriage ride back to the hotel. Lily teased her and Teresa looked for some telltale sign of similar infatuation in the twin's bright eyes. She found none. For his part, Tobias displayed no more symptoms of love-struck distraction.

As though he had been watching for their carriage, Lord Eads met them before the hotel. A boy holding a saddled horse waited nearby.

Lily and Effie told their brother of their activities while still standing on the street like the veriest hoydens, but Teresa couldn't bring herself to hurry them inside. She liked simply watching him. His whiskers were gone, leaving his jaw smooth and hard. A new coat stretched across his wide shoulders, his buckskins were fine, his boots shone, and his cravat was beautifully starched. He looked like a gentleman. But even without his rough Highland patina he made her pulse quicken.

"Are you coming or going, my lord?" she said as the others finally climbed the stairs to go inside.

He was staring at the hotel door through which his sisters had disappeared. "What did ye do to Abby?"

"I don't mind it that you have just ignored my question. I know you are discourteous to me because you don't like me. As for Abigail, I did nothing. The bookseller did. We stopped at the bookshop, which apparently she has already visited several times. I think they've developed a *tendre* for each other."

He turned his beautiful gaze upon her. "I niver said I didna like ye."

Her heart stumbled. "Then why do you speak to me as

you do? And why didn't you come to the park with us yesterday or to Lady B's today?"

He shook his head. "Yer a meddlesome woman."

"You've just insulted me again."

"I've no tact, Miss Finch-Freeworth."

"That isn't true. At least, not when you speak to your sisters. You are gracious and solicitous with them. It's only with me that you are rude. You are trying to frighten me off."

"Mebbe."

"Well you cannot. Not yet, at least. Now you owe me on our wager, my lord."

His cheek creased. "Aye?"

"Abigail and the bookseller." She lifted a forefinger. "That is one. I demand payment."

"They're no betrothed yet." His eyes twinkled.

"Not *yet*." She couldn't help smiling. "But clearly they *like* each other. I thought . . ."

"Ye thought to collect in advance?"

She was a little breathless. He stood close and she could not now hear the carriages passing or the shouts of an apple vendor on the corner over the pounding of her heart. "I hoped you might consider it."

"What? Here in the street?" he said in a low voice.

Yes. "In private, if you will."

"I will."

"You *will*?"

"I'm a man o' my word, miss." His mouth tilted up at one side.

"Would you say my name again?" she breathed.

"Miss Finch-Freeworth."

"Teresa, that is."

The twinkle in his eyes seemed entirely for her. "That wouldna be proper, would it?"

"Perhaps not, but I should like it quite a lot."

He moved a half step closer. "What have ye got in that bonnie head o' yers, lass, that makes ye believe ye've got leave to make demands as ye do?"

Dreams. Hopes. The desperate wish for somebody to understand her. "I am a distant relation to the king and imperiousness is in my blood."

"I dinna believe ye."

"Hm." She could not hold his gaze any longer. "Lord Eads, Mr. Yale says you can be trusted with a woman's safety," she said to her gloved fingers twined together. "But, it is the most curious thing, you see: It turns out that I do not feel in the least bit safe with you."

"That surprises ye?"

"Eighteen months ago I thought I knew . . . *something*. Even the other day when I went to your flat I thought I did. But the more I see of you the less . . . the less . . ."

"The less like a game it seems to ye."

She looked up. His handsome face was sober.

"No," she said. "It was never a game. Only . . . I wish you would speak to me."

"I'm speaking to ye nou."

"About something that matters. About something real."

He did not look at her as though she were queer. He did not scowl or frown or shake his head in confusion like everybody in Harrows Court Crossing always did when she spoke her heart.

"I did remember ye," he said quietly. "Hou can a man forget the sweetest smile he's ever seen?"

Oh. "Sweetest?"

His gaze traced her features. "Aye."

"Why did you pretend you didn't recognize me?"

"I wanted ye to go away. I want ye to go away nou. I'm praying ye'll go away o' yer own accord so I willna have to make ye."

"I cannot," she said through the clog in her throat. "I made a promise to your sisters."

He paused a moment. "Will ye have a ride aboot the park?" He gestured to the boy with the horse.

She blinked in surprise. "With you?"

"Aye."

"Now?"

His cheek dented again. "Aye."

"I haven't got a mount here, and I am not dressed for it."

"Tomorrow morning, then?"

"My lord, are you . . ." It was not possible, not after what he'd said. "Are you *courting* me?"

He laughed. "Ye've no patience for uncertainty, do ye, lass?"

"Please don't call me lass. And no. But . . . *are* you?"

"I anly wish to thank ye for the day ye've given ma sisters."

She sucked in her disappointment. "In that case I had better go inside and see what's what. The day I gave them wasn't quite ideal." Teresa started up the steps. The earl followed.

She halted two steps above him. "Lady Beaufetheringstone is holding a ball three evenings from tonight. Will you escort your sisters?" She fully expected him to decline this invitation above all. To him there could be no good in returning to the place she had first seen him.

"Aye, I'll do it," he said, took the two steps in one, and looked down at her. "Teresa Finch-Freeworth o' Brennon Manor in Harrows Court Crossing," he said quietly, as though savoring the syllables upon his tongue. "Ye've no idea the sort o' man I am or the deeds I've done."

"Then either you will have to tell me and allow me to make my own judgments, or I shall have to judge you according to the deeds you do now. Shan't I?"

He shook his head but he offered his arm. She laid her hand upon it.

"There," she said as briskly as she could. "This isn't so hard, is it?"

Duncan wanted to laugh. "Managing female," he muttered.

"Barbarian Scot."

"Saucy—"

"I asked you not to call me lass."

"Ye asked me to marry ye too, but I havena done that either, have I?"

"Not *yet*."

An expensive carriage with wheels rimmed in red, shining panels, and a matched quartet drew up on the street behind them. A young fellow disembarked. Without showy display, the diamond lodged in his neck cloth and the cut and tailoring of his garments proclaimed his wealth. He paused to speak with his coachman.

She drew away from Duncan and went to the porter at the door. "Who is that gentleman?"

"That's Mr. Reginald Baker-Frye of the Baker-Fryes of Philadelphia, miss," the porter confided with a weighty nod.

"Who are the Baker-Fryes?"

"Money, miss. Piles of merchant gold. Father just passed on and this one inherited the lot. Here to see to business."

"Is his wife traveling with him?"

"Not married, miss." He scoffed. "Why should he be when he's got scores of servants? If I didn't need a missus to mend my stockings and cook my dinner, I'd be a single man too."

Duncan watched in alarm. A wealthy young man had dropped down as if from heaven. He could see the gears turning in her mind, storing every detail.

"Thank you for that enlightening information," she said, and with a quirk of her pretty pink lips went into the parlor and ordered tea.

Her brother sat with a paper on his knee, the only person present other than a tiny grey-haired lady dressed in black. Sorcha entered and took up her cup with a snap of her narrow wrist that dashed tea across Duncan's dearly acquired new breeches.

"Oh," she said with a sharp flash of her eyes. "Pardon, brither."

His other sisters entered and conversation turned to ball gowns. He left. There were limits to his dedication to his mission.

In the foyer he passed the wealthy young American.

"Sir," Baker-Frye said with a nod, then glanced into the parlor. His steps faltered. Duncan followed his astonished gaze to Moira standing near the doorway. She cast down her eyes and curtsied to him.

Baker-Frye drew his hat off and bowed from his waist. "Madam."

"Guidday, sir." She lifted her lashes with a shy smile.

Finally the American dragged his gaze away and ascended the stairs.

Poor fellow. It happened to most men when they first saw Moira. But Duncan had never before seen his diffident sister respond.

He glanced back at Miss Finch-Freeworth. Her eyes shone as she transferred her attention from Moira to him. She wiggled her cinnamon brows and took a breath of obvious satisfaction that swelled her bosom above the modest neckline of her gown.

The air abruptly seemed thin indoors.

Tomorrow he would renew his attempts at distracting her from the wager. For today, he'd concede defeat.

Chapter Six

He called for her too early, he suspected. But he didn't want to miss the opportunity to distract her from her mission today.

Straightening his cravat as he waited for the door of Yale's house to open, he knew he was a fool. He'd spent half the night thinking of her pretty smile, lily pad eyes that could laugh with a twinkle, magnificent bosom, and round behind. He'd spent the other half of the night deep in dreams that upon waking had him hot and uncomfortable.

He was early because he wanted to see her.

Twenty-six days. He could bear this for twenty-six days.

A footman led him to a parlor where Miss Finch-Freeworth was perched upon the edge of a straight-back chair before a writing table, her head bent to her page.

"Lord Eads," the footman said and withdrew.

She jerked around, her lush pink lips making an O.

"My lord! You came this morning!"

No. But if he had to witness her creamy breasts jumping against her bodice many more times he'd be hard pressed to resist the temptation for that sort of relief. The lush circle of her lips didn't help any.

"Guidday, Miss Finch-Freeworth." He bowed. His waistcoat was tight across his chest, his shoulders were cramped in the coat, and he despised top boots. But he'd not go about like a ruffian and shame his sisters or this good-hearted lass—this tempting, outrageous lass who knew far too much about a woman's carnal needs than an unmarried lady should.

Hastily she dashed sand across her work then covered the page.

"Have you come to invite me to ride?" She glanced at his ensemble, lingering for a moment on the fall of his breeches, and her cheeks took on the hue of a ripe peach. Her gaze snapped up.

"What're ye writing?" His voice sounded rough.

"You've done that thing again, where you ignore what I have asked and ask me a question instead."

"Aye, I've come to take ye riding." Though he'd prefer a different sort of riding than the sort she had in mind.

Her attention flicked momentarily to his breeches again, then swiftly up. Her pretty green eyes were wide.

Perhaps she did have that sort of riding in mind.

He tried to find his brain. Despite his better judgment, he moved toward her. "What're ye writing?" he repeated.

"Oh." She waved her fingertips over the pages dismissively. "Nothing really."

"Poetry?"

"Poetry?"

He halted close enough to see that the rosy glow had suffused her neck and the soft globes of her breast above her gown too. He dragged his gaze upward.

"Leddies always seem to enjoy poetry."

"Not this lady."

"'Tis a relief." *Relief.* Nowhere near in sight. Not the sort he most needed. He shouldn't have come. She bit her pretty pink lip and flicked the tip of her tongue to moisten it and Duncan nearly groaned aloud.

"Why?" she said, her eyes glimmering now. "Since you claim you are not courting me, you needn't write me poetry."

"Ye've a clever tongue, Miss Finch-Freeworth." A tongue he'd like to see more of. But if he was imagining a virgin's tongue in action, clearly he'd been celibate for far too long. "An I dinna claim I'm no courting ye. I'm in fact no courting ye."

"Then if you will await me here, my lord, I will go change into my riding dress and call for my mount to be saddled so that you can take me riding in a decidedly un-courting-like manner." With a quick smile she curtsied and crossed the parlor, leaving in her wake a light scent of lemon.

For a moment he allowed himself to enjoy her scent. He would never again let himself come close enough to her to indulge his senses entirely. In the flat he'd made the mistake of touching her skin. He'd not do that again.

He glanced down at the writing table at the blank page with which she'd covered her writing. He looked back toward the door. It stood open, but if she were anything like most of his sisters she'd be at least a half hour preparing to go out.

The temptation was too great. He could never know her intimately. This could be his only opportunity to know her at least privately. And he'd committed much worse crimes for much worse reasons in the past.

He brushed the cover sheet aside. Her hand was neat, with a feminine curl to the capitals and a light freedom in the stroke. A peculiar sensation stirred beneath his waistcoat. He liked her hand. It was like her.

Her prose was light and clever, yet with the same warmth and animation that shone in her spring eyes. The lines told of a village matron who tended toward gossip and her two daughters, and their adventure ordering teacakes for the Ladies of Harpers Crest Cove Auxiliary Benefit. Their series of mishaps was amusing, the characters were drawn with wit and an eye toward satire that was, however, ultimately compassionate. He pushed the page aside and read the one beneath. Then he covered them and went to the window.

She appeared at the door minutes later. Her voluptuous figure was encased in a skirt and short coat the color of sunrise with a crisp white shirt beneath and a jaunty little hat adorning her hair. "I'm ready."

"Yer luvely."

Her cheeks glowed. He shouldn't have said it. He shouldn't be thinking it. He shouldn't be imagining how much he would enjoy removing that pretty dress from her curves one item at a time.

"Thank you, my lord. My horse is also ready. Are you?"

No. Once she mounted, her gown would be tucked around that round behind and he'd never have a chance—not at ignoring his body's reaction to her or at relief. He hadn't thought ahead of the potential dangers of this outing. It was possible he hadn't been thinking at all since the moment she had appeared in his flat and proposed marriage to him.

"Aye. I'm ready." He set his jaw and went forward to suffer through the most torturous ride in the park he had ever thoroughly enjoyed.

Teresa stood at the edge of Lady Beaufetheringstone's gorgeously appointed ballroom immersed in the golden glow of sparkling chandelier candles and glittering champagne glasses, and allowed herself a silent breath of relief. The orchestra cheerfully sawed out the notes of a country dance and guests stepped to the tune amidst the laughter and chatter of those watching. It was a magical evening and Teresa was barely even bothered by the conspicuous absence of a reneging Scottish earl.

Only that morning when he had escorted her and her sisters to the shops where they encountered no gentlemen except one portly popinjay entirely arrayed in puce, the earl had promised he would attend the ball tonight.

Faithless barbarian. But he owed her nothing yet. Mr. Baker-Frye had taken up Moira in his carriage to the park, and the bookseller had personally delivered a rare volume to Abigail at the hotel. Otherwise, despite a sennight of hard work altering gowns and schooling Lily and Effie on proper behavior, bachelors had not been banging down the Eads ladies' door.

Tonight, however, that was being corrected.

"You did it," Tobias said beside her.

"I did it," she agreed.

Earlier, as the seamstress sewed darts in the bodice of Teresa's white muslin so it would hug Effie's smaller bosom,

Elspeth had complained about the expense of the gown that Diantha lent her. She would not don it until Diantha assured her that much of the income from Mr. Yale's estate went toward the plight of suffering children in the Welsh mines and only some of it toward pretty clothes. Mollified, Elspeth allowed Annie to affix a chain of cameos around her long neck.

Sorcha had refused to attend the ball. But her sisters were all gowned and coiffed beautifully, even Abigail, whose cheeks glowed as she slipped away to Lady B's library. Lily and Effie were giggling at the refreshment table, their dance partners waiting attendance upon them. Moira was surrounded by young gentlemen, Lady B in their midst making introductions. And Una and Elspeth were dancing.

Teresa could not have prayed for better.

"Why aren't you dancing?" Tobias asked. "And where is Eads? I thought he'd meant to attend."

"I did," the earl said behind her.

She pivoted. He wore a black cutaway coat, gorgeously arranged neck cloth, and dark waistcoat, with a drape of blue and black plaid pinned to his shoulder. The kilt that fell to his knees revealed his muscular calves.

"My lord." Teresa curtsied somewhat unsteadily. He bowed with great elegance. No one watching could have imagined that their chance encounter eighteen months ago in this very ballroom had resulted in a scandalous secret wager.

Una approached with Elspeth.

"Ladies, you dance charmingly," Tobias said.

"I occasionally allou maself a country dance for the benefit it affords the lungs and heart," Elspeth said. "'Tis like a bracing walk across a meadow."

"I daresay," Tobias said pleasantly. "But what of the minuet or quadrille?"

"Or—heaven forbid—the waltz?" Una said.

Lady Elspeth paled. "Niver the waltz."

"Perhaps Lady Lily would like to waltz," Teresa said to her brother. "She mentioned her fondness for it just this afternoon," she invented.

"A lady after my own heart," Tobias said with a smile. "Do you enjoy the waltz too, Lady Una?"

"Verra much, sir."

He offered his arm. "Then it's lucky the orchestra seems to be in accord with our preferences." He led her away.

Teresa felt the earl's attention on her as she looked toward his youngest sisters. Effie had a cup of punch in each hand. Lily was laughing gaily.

"What're they doing there?" Elspeth said. "Effie's cheeks be aflame, like last Christmas when she took too much . . . *Ach*, Lord's mercy. Brither, ye'll wish to see to this," she said ominously and set off toward the twins.

"What happened last Christmas?" Teresa asked.

"Whiskey."

"I see. But Lady B is only serving punch tonight, so Effie is safe."

"Why are ye trying to throw Lily at yer brither's head?"

She snapped her eyes up. "I—That is . . ."

Amusement creased his cheek and his hair hung loosely. She wanted to reach up and touch it to test if it was as silky as it looked. He was a remarkably well-made man and ladies all around them were staring from behind their unfurled fans.

"He seems to like her," she said.

"Be ye such a fine judge o' a man, then?"

"Apparently not, for I thought you would not come this evening."

"I'm a man o' ma w—"

"Word. Yes, you've said that. Still, I will forgive your lateness if you ask me to dance."

"I dinna dance. But there be plenty o' swains here for ye to chuise from."

"I cannot dance with those gentlemen. I consider myself betrothed."

He grinned. "Yer mad."

"I probably am. It must be all that country air from bracing walks. It does strange things to the head." Like make her believe she could coerce a Scottish lord into wedding her. She'd made an enormous mistake. But at least she was helping seven young women find the loves of their lives, even if she would never be allowed her own. "But do look over there, my lord." She gestured toward Moira dancing with Mr. Baker-Frye. "Aren't they gorgeous together? He is staying at the King Harry."

"Is he?"

"Oh yes. He is a merchant from Philadelphia. Fabulously wealthy, of course. Lady B was happy to include him on the guest list. She isn't particular about a gentleman's pedigree when he's as handsome as Mr. Baker-Frye. And he really is so handsome, don't you think?"

He lowered his brow.

"Are you scowling because I arranged their introduction or because you cannot say whether or not he is handsome?"

"I'm no scowling." His eyes sparkled. "'Tis ma thoughtful look."

"I see. Well then, do bend your thoughts to how Mr. Baker-Frye appears more than halfway smitten. This ball is turning out to be a fabulous success for your sisters, it seems."

A crash sounded from the direction of the punch bowl. They both looked around.

Not from the direction of the punch bowl—in fact, from the punch bowl itself.

Shards and chunks of crystal were everywhere. Lily's eyes and mouth were wide in dismay. Effie's maidenly white skirt was awash in punch.

"Guid lord, Lily!" rang Effie's lilting Scottish brogue over the orchestra's lilting Austrian waltz. "Couldna ye wait till I'd anither cup afore ye went and spilt it all over me?" She burst into peals of laughter.

Elspeth snagged the lobe of Effie's right ear and gave it a good shake. Lily grabbed Elspeth's wrist, lost her balance, and thumped to her bottom in the puddle of punch.

All around fans fluttered at top speed. Dozens of pairs of eyes stared.

The waltz lilted on.

Teresa lifted her chin, averted her gaze from the dark scowl of the large, handsome man beside her, and walked toward the refreshment table.

While she'd never been clumsy herself, Teresa did not think Lily deserved Elspeth's stern lecture or Effie's drunken rehash of every detail of the disaster as they drove home.

Tobias had accompanied Una, Moira, and Abigail in the other carriage, so Teresa disembarked before the King Harry, bid the sisters goodnight, and joined her brother for the ride home. Lord Eads had ridden, and she was for once glad not to see him and bear the consequences of what she had allowed to happen.

Allowed. As if she could control seven strong-willed Scotswomen! She would have better success finding husbands for every unwed lady in Harrows Court Crossing, including the elderly spinster sisters who lived above the parsonage and the butcher's old sow. Except herself, of course.

"It was going so well," she sighed.

"They're new to it yet," Tobias said easily. "They'll learn. And Lady B didn't mind it."

She peered at him. "You seem cheerful. Did you enjoy yourself?" Despite Lily's mishap?

"I did." He turned his face toward the window and the light from the street lamp without illumined his drawn brow.

"Toby? Are you regretting having given your consent to this project after all?"

"No. It's only . . ." He shook his head. "It's nothing to worry your head over. Ah, look, we have arrived. You must be fagged to death." He handed her out and sent the carriage on its way.

"Won't you ride home?"

He took a deep breath and stood tall and square shouldered on the walkway. "I could use a stroll to—well, to clear my head. And my rooms aren't far. Now you go on and I'll watch you inside."

She went onto her tiptoes and bussed him lightly on the cheek. "I don't know what is amiss with you, but I do hope it will be well in the morning."

He nodded shortly. She went up the steps and he waved as the door closed behind her.

"What time is it, Michael?" she asked the sleepy footman as he drew the night bolt.

"Half past one, miss."

"I suppose Mrs. Yale has long since gone to bed?"

"Yes, miss."

She would've liked a cozy chat with Diantha. But the baby was waking her friend at all hours; it would not be fair to bother her now. And of course Diantha might not be alone in bed. She was fortunate enough to be married to a man she loved and who loved her in return.

"Thank you, Michael. I will sit in the parlor for a bit. I'll put out the candles on my way to bed."

"G'night, miss." He bowed and disappeared into the back of the house.

She took up a candle and went into the parlor to the writing desk, and drew her latest pages out of the drawer. A few minutes working on her newest story would cheer her. Freddie would split his seams when he read about the blacksmith and curate's wife getting trapped in the old cider house. A smile twitched her lips.

The parlor door opened. "Miss, a gentleman is here calling on you," the footman said with a twisted brow. "Should I turn him away?"

"A gentleman? At this hour?"

"Says he's a lord, miss."

She ran to the window and peeked through the draperies. Her heart did a miserable little thud.

"He should not come inside," she said because she knew it to be true but also because she could not bear to face what was about to come. "I will go to the door. You can go ahead to bed now. I'll bolt it after he leaves."

"Yes, miss."

The Earl of Eads looked as handsome in the candlelight slicing through the cracked open door as he did beneath the brilliant illumination of a ballroom chandelier.

"You needn't say a thing," she said with heavy resignation. "I already know."

"Invite me in, woman," he only said.

"I really shouldn't."

"Ye will, nivertheless."

Her throat was thick as she drew the door open. She clasped her hands before her, the pale pink lace reticule that matched her gown still dangling from her wrist, albeit limply; it had soaked up Effie's punch.

"All right," she said dully. She'd never imagined defeat would come so early and in quite this manner. "Say what you have come to say." She wanted to shout, "No!" She had feared this moment—the moment when he would tell her that the game had been amusing but now he was putting a halt to it.

"I came to tell ye why I was late to the ball," he said.

She blinked. "You did?"

He glanced toward the open parlor door. "What're ye doing awake?"

"I was . . . That is, I was . . ."

"Writing a story?"

Her heart tripped. "What?"

"I read yer story th'ither day while ye were upstairs." He stood solid and powerful and entirely unapologetic before her.

Heat suffused her cheeks. "You should not have."

"It was a fine piece."

"You liked it?"

"Aye. Verra much. Ye've got a talent, lass."

She could not withhold her smile. "Thank you. I'm glad you enjoyed it. So glad that I won't even chastise you for calling me lass."

His beautiful blue eyes glimmered with candlelight. "I beg yer pardon."

"You are forgiven. Again." She felt wonderfully warm and much too happy and he was far too handsome and she was thoroughly infatuated.

"Mr. Abel Brown paid a call on me this eve."

"What?" She clutched her reticule between her fingers. "That is—who?"

"The proprietor o' Brown & Cheaver Booksellers."

"The *bookseller?*"

Lord Eads took a step toward her. "Seems he wishes to court Abigail."

"He does?" She was short of breath.

He halted so that mere inches separated them. "He said he niver imagined I'd allou such a thing, but he begged for her hand."

"Did—" Her heart was performing complicated pirouettes. "Did you give it?"

"Aye, I gave it. Who woulda thought Abby'd be the first?" Affection played across his face. He truly cared for his sisters' happiness.

"Do you consider a bookseller a suitable match for your sister?"

"He's a guid man wi' a steady income and a fine shop. If she's got no trouble wi' it, I dinna."

"You must be thrilled," she babbled because his eyes had taken on a gleam of pure intentionality and now that the moment she'd been dreaming of for eighteen months was finally happening *she had no idea what to do.* "I must congratulate you on this happy news, my lord."

"'Tis I that should congratulate ye."

"Oh, no. I really didn't have anything to do with it." *What was she saying?* "They'd already met be—"

He slipped his hand into her hair.

"Oh!" she sighed. His touch didn't feel like she had dreamed it. It felt *infinitely better,* strong and warm and confident, and as he bent his head she got dizzy on his scent of exotic spices. Her eyelids fluttered down. "I have never kissed a man who was wearing a skirt before," she whispered.

"'Tis no a skirt."

"Be that as it may . . ."

"But ye have kissed a man?" he said over her lips.

"Once."

"What was he wearing?"

He was laughing at her again, even at this moment. Or rather, *with* her. She liked it. It made her heart feel light and deliciously free.

"Muddy boots and a coat that smelled of shotgun smoke."

"Bounder."

"Definitely a bounder. He cornered me in the gunroom after he returned from shooting with my brothers. I thought I would give it a try, to see what all the fuss was about, you know," she said airily.

"What did ye discover?" He was drawing this out, to torture her or because he didn't wish to do it. But he had come in the middle of the night to pay his debt on the wager. Perhaps he was as eager as she.

"Discover?" she breathed.

"Aboot the fuss?"

"That it was overrated."

His thumb stroked the tender ridge of her cheek. "Then he wasna doing it right."

"Are you going to prove that now?"

"Aye."

Her lips were sweet. Sweeter than he'd imagined. Sweeter than any woman's lips he'd ever tasted. He caught her soft sigh in his mouth and stroked his thumb across her buttercream cheek dusted with pale cinnamon freckles. He tasted her again, this time longer, deeper, and her lips were soft responding, then eager.

His cock stirred.

He broke the contact. "Ye've anly been kissed once afore? By the bounder?"

"Yes." Her breaths were quick against his lips. "Only that once."

"Ye've got a knack for it."

"I've thought about it quite a lot," she said shakily. "Was that all I get? That one?"

"That wasna quite one, nou was it?"

She shook her head.

He took her lips again, this time more fully, and she responded more fully. He wrapped his hand around the back of her neck and urged her lips apart. She opened to him upon an intoxicating sigh. He traced the edge of her satiny lower lip with the tip of his tongue and she gasped then sought him with her tongue. Her soft, pink, wet, agile tongue that lately he'd been imagining doing things no lady's tongue should ever do—things to him. Her tongue that tasted like sugared lemons and tangled with his, eagerly drawing him inside her, urging him deeper with each kiss.

He should halt this. He should have already halted this. He shouldn't have come. He shouldn't be in this house in the middle of the night with this woman's mouth beneath his. But she'd sparkled in that ballroom like sunshine, and he'd wanted to take her into his arms and give her that dance. When his sisters embarrassed themselves she hadn't blinked a lash but saw to the fiasco calmly and serenely.

Now she was eager in his hands, seeking his caresses with her mouth, and hot inside. Good lord, she was feverishly hot. She'd be hot everywhere inside, and damp, and virginally tight. She was going to make some lucky man a fine wife indeed. Some *very lucky* man.

Her hand slipped across his chest and pressed against his heart.

Duncan choked and set her away from him.

"Payment delivered," he said gruffly.

She blinked dazed eyes. Her soft pink lips were moist and so lush it hurt to look at them. It hurt to look at *her.* It hurt to know how it felt to have her hand on his chest.

She nodded. She didn't offer him a saucy quip or glimmering grin, and that was the worst of all.

"Guid nicht." He reached for the door, swung it open, and escaped into the darkness to which he was well accustomed.

Chapter Seven

Teresa went to the hotel after breakfast. She found Elspeth poking out a tune on the pianoforte in the parlor, Moira embroidering, Abigail in her corner reading, and the elderly woman in black staring silently out the window.

Abigail lifted her head. "Duncan's gone to the shop wi' Una."

"Where are Lily and Effie?"

Elspeth plunked a minor chord. "Ma most foolish an heedless sister is suffering the consequences o' her indulgence."

"Effie's got a megrim," Abigail explained.

"I shouldn't wonder at it." Teresa went to her. "May I offer you congratulations?"

Abigail's cheeks grew ruddy. "Mr. Brown's engaged to take me walking in the park this afternoon. Duncan told me what he intends to ask me."

She squeezed Abigail's hand. "I am so happy for you."

"At least Abigail has a sense o' propriety," Elspeth said sourly.

"Oh, Speth, don't go naggin' this early in the morn," Effie said from the doorway with a hangdog face. "I canna bear it." She turned a wary look on Teresa.

Teresa went to her. "A cup of coffee, a small beer, a glass of water, and sleep sleep sleep."

Effie's red eyes widened.

"Without delay," Teresa said. "But first tell me where to find your twin."

"She's hiding," Effie said with less defiance.

"Where?"

"In the kitchen. 'Tis where she always hides."

In the hotel's expansive kitchen scents of roasting meat, simmering delicacies, and baking cake mingled with the clatter of plates and cups as the scullery maids cleaned up from breakfast. Steam rose over copper pots on the fires.

Tucked in a corner by the pantry the youngest Eads lady was carefully measuring cups of flour into a sifter, cranking the flour into a bowl then pouring it back into the bin. Then she began the process all over again. Her hair was tucked beneath a kerchief and her cheeks were smudged with flour powder. Her eyes were lackluster.

"Oh, guidday, Teresa," she said dully.

"It appears that you are busy with some industry. May I help?"

"Oh, ye needn't fret that I'll make trouble here. I've niver spilt a grain o' flour or nutmeg in ma life."

"Really? How wonderful. I am terribly clumsy in the kitchen." Not a complete fabrication.

"*Sacre bleu!*"

In the doorway stood a compact man with black eyes, a

neat moustache, and a fastidious pinstriped coat. "What are these womens in my kitchen?" he exclaimed with a Gallic gesture of contempt.

"Oh!" Lily dropped the measuring cup into the bowl. "Oh," she said more miserably. "I beg yer pardon, sir." Her pretty eyes sought Teresa's for a brief, anguished moment. Then she hurried past the Frenchman and out.

He stared after her.

Teresa went to him. "How to you do, monsieur. I am Miss Finch-Freeworth, a friend of several of the guests in this hotel."

"Marcel Le Coq, *a votre service*, mademoiselle." He bowed and glanced out the door again.

"What a well-appointed kitchen you have. I have heard raptures about your dinners."

"Mais, bien sur," he dismissed the compliment and sniffed the air. "But what is this? I did not give permission for the cakes to be baked today. Agathe? Agathe!"

A kitchen maid snapped to attention. "Monsieur, it was the other lady. She'd done it when I was serving breakfast to the guests upstairs and I thought as since they were so pretty I'd let them have their time in the oven."

Monsieur Le Coq narrowed his eyes and stalked to the oven. With exaggerated disdain he wrenched open the door, grabbed up a cloth, and pulled forth the tray of cakes. He dropped it onto the counter. With the tip of his forefinger and thumb he plucked up one, brought it to his nose to sniff, and nibbled it.

His face relaxed. "C'*est bon.*" He took another bite. "C'*est magnifique.*" He cut Teresa a suspicious glance. She shrugged.

He ignored her after that and she went to find Lily. But the downcast girl had escaped to the park with Sorcha.

Finding Moira still in the parlor, Teresa settled into a cozy chat from which she emerged confident that of all the beaux with whom the beauty had danced the previous night she preferred the Philadelphian. Modest and reticent, she said nothing to reveal this, but Teresa discerned in her smile a special glow when she spoke of Mr. Baker-Frye. She applauded herself for a deed well done.

Teresa ferried her new friends from London drawing room to drawing room, using her every connection (including silly Aunt Hortensia) to put them in the way of gentlemen and mothers of eligible bachelors. Occasionally gratifying but more often dispiriting, these adventures were followed by visits to the bookshop and the confectioner's for ices to cheer everybody up.

"Ye canna blame yerself, Teresa," Una said. "'Tis the way o' the world. No gentleman wants a leddy without a fine marriage portion lest she be a beauty."

"I beg to disagree, my lady," Tobias said. "Some gentlemen value a fine temperament and intelligence in a bride over other considerations."

"Gentlemen like you, Toby," Teresa said. "Won't you invite some of your new friends from the War Office to join us on our next outing?"

"Perhaps we should ask Lady Una if she would like that," he said.

"I should, thank ye." She smiled.

Optimistic plans aside, Teresa's distress over her failure to find suitable husbands for the earl's sisters grew daily. Surprisingly, she found some relief from that distress in the regular company of the earl himself. He escorted them to take in the sculptures at the museum and on another day to the Tower of London. He hired a box at the theater, and a drive or ride with him and one or two of his sisters in the park during the quiet morning hours became habitual.

She was, however, not once alone in his company and he did not show any desire to see her alone. She longed to renew the embrace he had given her after Lady B's ball and had every confidence that he wished quite the opposite. He could not have escaped that moment more swiftly, leaving her lips tingling and fantasies flying.

At the end of the wager's second sennight, during which the Eads ladies met a total of three new gentlemen—a pair of octogenarians at the museum and Mr. Smythe, Tobias's new friend from the War Office—she managed to find Diantha at home one afternoon both awake and alert.

"Please, Di, will you finally tell me about Lord Eads?"

"He has done crimes," her friend said firmly.

"He wouldn't be the only one in this room," her husband muttered from behind his news journal. Wyn lowered the paper to cast his wife a slanted look. Diantha rolled her eyes at him.

"Crimes?" Teresa said. "As in acts that a *criminal* commits?"

Diantha nodded ominously.

Teresa felt shaky. This she had not expected. "When?"

"Years ago," Wyn supplied.

"T, I simply cannot like this program," Diantha repeated

for the hundredth time in the fortnight. "Why can't you fix your interest on a gentleman with a less dangerous past? There are plenty to be found about town."

"Come now, my dear," her husband said gently. "A man should always be given a second chance, shouldn't he?"

They shared a private, expressive look that left Teresa feeling peculiarly achy.

"Eads is fortunate to have won your admiration, Teresa," Wyn said. "I only hope he is worthy of it."

"Would you like it if we invited him and his sisters to dinner, T?" Diantha said hesitantly.

Teresa bit her lip. "I thought neither of you liked him."

"We should invite them," Wyn said.

As Diantha and Wyn's household was often filled with misfits and orphans anyway, the couple warmly welcomed to dinner Tobias, Abigail's bookseller, and Mr. Baker-Frye along with the seven Eads ladies. Upon coming face to face, Mr. Yale and Lord Eads moved away from the group, engaged in several minutes of private conversation during which both their jaws seemed very tight. Then Wyn laughed, the earl cracked a slow grin, and after that the party began in earnest.

Diantha swiftly—sneakily—sat Teresa far away from Lord Eads at the table. Teresa tried not to watch him from a distance and failed. When she was in company with him it was astoundingly difficult not to stare at his lips and relive the effect they'd had upon hers, not to mention the effect they'd had on parts quite a bit deeper inside her. While she was staring, those deep parts would become remarkably hot and agitated, and her cheeks would grow warm. Then she would have to look away from him, which was a shame because she liked looking at him. She liked listening to him. She liked watching his cheek crease when he was amused and his eyes twinkle.

It was all terribly inconvenient and enormously frustrating.

After dinner the gentleman remained in the dining room at their port while in the drawing room Moira and Una played a duet on the pianoforte as Diantha poured tea. Teresa was pondering how the evening was decidedly not what her life would be like as the future Mrs. Waldon when the earl came to her side.

"'Tis the halfway mark," he said quietly. "Are ye ready to call it quits? Admit ye bit aff more than ye could chew?"

She peeked at him from the corner of her eye and saw precisely what she wished to chew: his jaw. Then she would nibble his chin. Then she would move to his throat. The notion set off the familiar wild flutterings deep in her belly.

"No," she replied. "I have a fortnight yet." Mr. Baker-Frye had taken tea with Moira, each morning for three days in a row she had encountered him in the park, and he had accepted the invitation to dinner tonight with enthusiasm. It could not be long before an alliance happened there. One accomplished, one in the making, and only five to go. In a fortnight. "I will do it. Mark my words."

"'Tis a struggle to mark them when I canna think o' anything but the pretty lips that've spoken them."

Her mouth fell open. He made no pretense of looking elsewhere.

"I canna get yer flavor outta ma head, Miss Teresa Finch-Freeworth."

"Then kiss me again," she whispered. "Right now. There's an empty parlor just on the other side of that door."

"Ye like to drive a man as mad as yerself, dinna ye?" His voice was smiling and ever so slightly husky.

"Not intentionally." She held her breath. "What I would really like is to know more about you." She craned her neck to look into his face.

He was no longer smiling. "Ye must make an end to this wager."

"I shall. In a fortnight."

He moved away. She put on a genial face and laughed and chatted with everybody. But that night when Diantha and Wyn had gone to bed and the house was again dark, she stole down to the parlor and wrote a little piece she titled "The Maid Milliner of Harpers Crest Cove and the Trouble With Desire: A Story of Seed Cakes."

When she was finished she sanded it and tucked it into the drawer. The pile of pages seemed thinner than before. But she was weary and discouraged and not thinking perfectly straight. In the morning she would pull out all the stories and send a few to Freddie. He would laugh himself to pieces.

She went to bed telling herself that would be enough. It must be enough. It was all the real happiness she would ever have.

Duncan read the London journals. He knew as well as anybody that scandal was afoot at one of the town's rag sheets. The editor had hired a lady journalist and he was giving her a byline. Gossip was flying, but the column was already wildly popular.

It seemed to him that the London public would also enjoy satirical snippets of life in a provincial town written by a lady humorist. It so happened that he had several such stories in his possession now. So, after he spent the morning riding in the park with his sisters and the lady from Cheshire that made him forget his past, he paid a call on the offices of *The London Weekly*.

A woman with a rich fantasy life should have an outlet for it that did not involve ruining her future.

The weather grew warm and fine, and for a single day Teresa wanted nothing to do with searching fruitlessly for suitors. It seemed that everywhere Lord Eads escorted them, no eligible gentlemen were to be found anyway. She almost believed he was trying to sabotage his sisters' chances.

But if they were to engage in gentleman-scarce outings, one may as well be of her own creation. She made plans and called at the hotel to invite her friends.

"Lily's no been herself since the ball, an Effie's itching to make trouble again." Una took Teresa's arm as they went into the parlor. The same ancient little grey lady draped in black wool sat staring out the window.

"Good day, ma'am," Teresa said, then to Una: "I have something planned that should put both Lily and Effie to rights. I came to tell you."

"I've news first. Mr. Baker-Frye asked ma brither for Moira's hand this morn."

"But that was very quick!"

"She's verra beautiful." Una winked. "But I think he cares for her. For all that he's worth twenty thousand a year, he's a kind man. Moira says they agree on everything."

"Everything?"

"Everything."

"How remarkably dull and wonderful for them."

Una laughed.

With a light step, Teresa went around telling the sisters about her planned outing at week's end and bidding them all dress suitably for the outdoors. Moira's cheeks glowed.

"May I invite Mr. Baker-Frye, Teresa? He's fond o' growing things."

"Of course. What a merry party we will be."

Only Abigail and Lily could not be found, but Teresa suspected where to search for at least one of the missing sisters.

In the kitchen, quiet in the lull between breakfast and lunch preparations, Lily was arranging sprigs of fresh herbs about the edges of two dozen little chicken carcasses laid out on a roasting pan.

"Abby's gone back to the bookstore." She offered a game smile.

"Dearest Lily, you must pull yourself out of this brown study and—"

"*Qu'est-ce que*—What are you doing?" Monsieur Le Coq rushed forward from the doorway, throwing off his hat as he came.

"Dressing these capons," Lily said. "They look so much prettier this way. And they will taste divine."

"*Mais, vous—*" Then he looked up and his dark eyes opened in wonder. "*Mon ange,*" he whispered.

Lily cocked her head. "What does that mean?"

And so Hotel King Harry's exclusive French chef was obliged to translate for the seventeen-year-old Scottish angel who had appeared in his kitchen days earlier for so brief a moment that he thought he'd imagined her, though she'd left behind the most miraculous cakes he had ever tasted. He not only translated but he rhapsodized in a manner only the French could affect, with such mellifluous praise that Lily's eyes were shining by the time he finished.

"Monsieur, yer a poet," she said brightly. Then more hesitantly: "Might I make cakes again today? Or mebbe a pudding?"

"I would be honored, mademoiselle!" he said with a flourishing bow that encompassed the entirety of his realm.

Lily beamed.

Disconcerted, Teresa left them to their cakes and chickens. She did not recall ever seeing Lily's eyes shine at Tobias quite like they had at the fastidious little French chef. Bemused and not liking where her thoughts brought her, she set off on foot for her brother's flat four blocks away.

"Walk aboot wi' yer head in the clouds, lass, an yer likely to take a tumble."

She snapped her cloudy head up to see Lord Eads astride his beautiful big roan stallion on the street beside her.

"Good day, my lord. My head was not in the clouds but in the hotel with your sisters. Congratulations on your acquisition of another brother-in-law."

"Will ye claim ye'd no hand in that one too?" The shadow

cast by the brim of his hat fell across his eyes and she could not tell if he was smiling.

"No, for I did. Although they might have encountered each other in the corridor any day, it's true."

"Do ye niver have a maid wi' ye, Miss Finch-Freeworth?"

"Annie walked with me to the hotel but she was distracted by a footman, I think. I could not find her when I departed."

He dismounted and drew his horse toward her. "'Tis no way for a leddy to go aboot town. Alone."

"I am always alone, my lord." Even with Annie. *Painfully alone.* The only real friend she'd ever had in Harrows Court Crossing had gone away to school when she was only ten years old and then to war when she was fifteen, and until he inherited Brennon Manor from their father he was unlikely to return. Her three years at the Bailey Academy for Young Ladies had afforded her the dear friendship of Diantha, and lately she had grown deeply fond of Lady Una. But at home in Cheshire she had no one with whom to share her stories and dreams. "And I hardly see how a man who has committed crimes and kissed a lady in a foyer after midnight can lecture me on propriety."

"I wasna lecturing ye on propriety, but safety."

"Then what about the foyer?"

"A man o' honor pays his debts."

"And . . ." Something seemed to be caught in her throat. "The crimes?"

His horse scraped a hoof. A carriage rattled by. The sun tried to peek out from a cloud then lost courage and inched behind it again.

"I killed a man," he finally said.

This had not been part of Teresa's fantasy of the handsome Highlander.

"Was it a duel?"

"No."

"An accident?"

"Cold bluid." He seemed to study her. "Nou will ye cancel the wager, lass?"

"Why did you kill him?"

"Does it matter?"

"I don't know yet."

"I admire yer honesty."

"You admire one thing about me and it is my *honesty*?" She shook her head.

"'Tis no the anly thing aboot ye I admire."

A hesitant smile shaped her pretty lips that Duncan hadn't stopped thinking about in a sennight since he'd had them at his command.

"What else do you admire?" she asked.

"That ye dinna tolerate the unkindnesses others show ma sisters."

Her eyes widened.

"An I admire yer courage."

"Courage?"

"An yer brazen cheek."

"*Brazen cheek?*" A crease ticked the bridge of her nose. "Now then, my lord, I don't—"

"An hou ye pretend yer doing this all for yerself when 'tis clear ye thrive on helping others."

"I am doing it for myself."

"An I already told ye I admire the lips I kissed in that foyer."

Her eyes took on a slightly confused, sultry luster. "And I already told you that you may kiss them again if you wish. But despite your pretty words I don't think you do."

"Aye, I do."

For a moment she did not speak. Then: "I don't trust you."

A weight seemed to press upon his chest. "Years ago a blackguard enticed ma sister Miranda from home wi' fine promises, forced her into foul service in Lunnon, then left her on the street to die. That was the man I killed."

Her throat jerked. "I am sorry," she said softly. "More sorry for you than I can express." Then with an air of firm decision, she stepped away from him. "Come to the picnic tomorrow, my lord. If you are very well behaved I will let you again kiss these lips that you so admire." She set off, striding down the walkway alone, her coppery locks shimmering beneath her bonnet, leaving him bemused and wanting more.

He put his horse into a lad's keeping and went after her. Her eyes were wide when he took her hand and laid it upon his arm.

"What are you doing?"

"Escorting ye to wherever it is yer going."

"Is this only about your concern over my safety?"

"Aye," he lied. "'Tis anly that."

Chapter Eight

Friday dawned bright and clear, ideal for the picnic. Four carriages were loaded with Eads ladies, servants, and baskets of savories and sweets prepared by Diantha's cook. The gentleman rode alongside.

Ascot Manor, the estate of retired naval commander George Finch-Ascot, sat at the end of a spectacularly long drive miles outside of London. Its extensive grounds included a collection of Greek and Roman sculptures, vast gardens, and several famous hothouses.

Admiral and Mrs. Finch-Ascot were not in residence, the housekeeper informed them. But in his absence the admiral extended a warm welcome to his cousin and her friends, and begged them to enjoy the park at their leisure. A suitable spot for a picnic was agreed upon and the ladies set to laying out blankets and baskets.

Teresa chatted with everyone, and she studied Una for signs of interest in Toby's friends from the War Office. But she could not eat a morsel. Since the earl had escorted her to her brother's apartment building the previous day her stomach had been tied in knots. They had spoken nothing more of his violent and tragic past, instead mostly of Harrows Court Crossing and his sisters. She knew so little of him, all of it confusing, yet when he bid her adieu with a proper bow she only wanted to ask him to remain with her, to stretch the moments into hours and make it last.

He laughed at her quips and tales as though he understood them. He said he thought she was mad but he never actually treated her as though she were a curiosity merely to be tolerated. Except for his regular offers to end the wager prematurely, he gave her no sign of disliking her company.

Rather the contrary. When she spoke he often watched her lips but he never stared at her bosom.

She was more than halfway to falling in love with a man with a dark past who would never marry her.

Admiral Finch-Ascot's gardener appeared and offered a tour of the park's cultivated beds and impressive statuary. Teresa went gladly; she needed a moment away from the earl to order her feelings.

Her brother and Lady Una walked together. As the gardener led them about, every so often Una would lift her face and speak quietly to Tobias. For an hour he did not leave her side.

Teresa was standing at the back of the group, brow furrowed as she stared at Una and Tobias and considered what it might take in the next two hours to lead them to a secluded place and abandon them there, when a man's large hand covered her behind.

She gasped. But she knew whose hand it was, and she did not move.

"What are you doing?" she whispered nonsensically because she knew perfectly well what he was doing.

His hand slipped away. "Stroll wi' me," he said in that deep, slightly rough brogue that made her liquid inside.

They left the group and followed a path that meandered toward a hothouse. When they were well away from the group she could bear the suspense no longer. She snatched open the hothouse door, poked her head in, and beckoned to him. He followed her inside and closed the door in an oddly pensive manner. Then he walked to her amidst exotic blooms and broad-fingered fig leaves.

"Did you do that because of our wager or because you especially wanted to?" she said.

He offered her a roguish grin.

"Who is betrothed?" she asked.

"It seems ma sister Lily has a fancy to bake cakes."

"Wishing to bake cakes does not make her betrothed to be married, my lord."

"Her bridegroom says otherwise. This morn he signed a contract to purchase a bakery for her."

"He did?" She clapped in delight. "Well, I am immeasurably happy for her. Monsieur Le Coq seems like a . . . a . . . that is to say, he is a—"

"French chef."

Her stomach was all butterflies. The air in the hothouse was sweetly scented and warm. "Was that it?" she asked. "What you did back there? Was that the inappropriate touch I am to have?"

"It suits the terms o' yer wager."

"Our wager."

He moved close and the budding branches of a peach tree framed his handsome face and wide shoulders. "Our wager," he repeated.

"You startled me, you know. I am unaccustomed to men groping my behind."

His brows rose. "I should hope so."

"You sound like Lady Elspeth."

The twinkle she adored lit his eyes. "'Tis the first time anybody's accused me o' that, to be sure."

"About that inappropriate touch . . ." Her mouth was terribly dry. She licked her lips.

"Do that again," he said in a low voice.

"Do what again?"

"Lick yer lips."

She did it, and it felt like wicked sin to do it expressly for him.

He took her face in his hands and covered her mouth with his. It was certainly testament to his extraordinary skill in kissing that she experienced the descent of his hand in a sort of molten haze of pleasure. When his palm came to rest at the small of her back then slipped down to possess her buttock, this time thoroughly and securely, she heard herself moan into his mouth.

"I want to feel ye against me, Teresa Finch-Freeworth o' Brennon Manor at Harrows Court Crossing in Cheshire," he said huskily over her lips, his hand stroking her behind. "All o' ye."

"I—" She grabbed hold of his coat and nodded. "I believe the terms of the wager allow for that."

He drew her against him and it did not feel distasteful

like when the bounder had pushed her against the gunroom wall, but a little alarming and very good. His chest and thighs were hard and her breasts flattened as he crushed her against him. Nothing except resting on her belly had ever caused her breasts to do anything other than stick out too far, and then they always made it too uncomfortable to sleep. This was *not* uncomfortable. It was quite as though his broad chest and muscular arms had been made to cradle her breasts safely, securely, just as his hand was cradling her buttock. In imitation, her mouth seemed to want to make a home for his tongue, inviting him to enter her again and again, first gently, seeking, then with deeper, possessing thrusts that made her wild inside.

Twining her hands into his waistcoat, she let him bear her back against the hothouse wall, and at that moment was introduced to that particular hardness the likes of which Annie had been telling her about for years—a *masculine* hardness that told a woman a man was fully prepared for the marriage act.

But they were not married and were unlikely to become married. He was kissing her because she had invited him to do so with a wager, the terms of which were truly impossible to fulfill even given her early serendipitous success. And although he wanted her to go away and had in fact told her so in no uncertain terms, she was kissing him back and allowing him to press her thighs apart with his knee and massage her behind with his strong fingers until she was mad for some uncertain satisfaction. When his hands urged her hips against his she arced to him. For a fleeting instant she knew a frisson of gratification, an instant that made her seek it again. It felt *so good.* Far too good. Better than her wildest imaginings.

"*Oh*."

The rumble in his chest echoed her gasp. He kissed her neck, his mouth hot on her tender skin, and the humid air of summer bursting with life and sex surrounded her and filled her head and body with yearning. Six years of need, a young womanhood of frustrated passion desperate to find a mate, seemed to burst from her and fed itself into her clutching hands and her gasps of pleasure.

He held her against him and spoke at her throat. "Why did ye chuise me, Teresa?"

"Why did I—*Oh*." She nestled her hips into his kneading hands.

"I've nothing." He nipped at her lower lip and a tingling rush filled her belly. "No money." His hands bracketed her hips, his fingertips caressing, pleasing. "A crumbling castle. A brood o' wimmenfolk I canna even clothe properly. A benighted title no proud man would wish to claim." His voice was heavy with bewilderment and need. "Why me?"

She ran her palms along his arms, solid and bunched with tension, and groaned from the echoing tension deep in her. "I don't know."

His hands stilled. "Ye *dinna ken*?"

"I dinna ken!" She opened her eyes. "It was a fantasy, a dream, a make-believe story like the stories I always tell. But this time I told it to myself." The words stumbled from her tongue. "I saw you that night at the ball, and you were so far beyond my reach, and I invented it but I never expected it to come true. I don't really know how I actually went through with it, came to London and went to your flat and proposed to you. Propositioned you. It was a dream. An impossible dream. It still feels like a dream, for I cannot have possibly traveled so far from being the exceedingly proper wife of the local vicar to kissing an earl with a dark and violent past in a hothouse. It is unthinkable."

"'Tis anly a dream, yet ye've gone an done this to me?" His eyes seemed to plead and accuse at once. But he had done it all to her, taken her in his arms and touched her and made her need not some ephemeral taste of spring, but *him*. She wanted to be the spring ewe to his ram. She wanted to be the nectar in the bud to his hummingbird's probe. She wanted him to make her a woman in this hothouse. Now. Before it was too late and she had to box up her mating metaphors as well as her dreams and store them all away at the back of a closet forever.

His arms fell away from her and he stepped back. "The exceedingly proper wife o' the local vicar?" he said in a thick voice.

"Not yet. And *his* idea. And my parents'. Decidedly not mine." She shivered in revulsion.

"Ye'd be a poor match for a beadle."

"If by beadle you mean a vicar, I consider that a compliment." She lifted her hands to her flaming cheeks. "Now what?"

"Nou, Miss Teresa Finch-Freeworth," he said in his beautiful rolling brogue, a muscle contracting in his jaw. "Ye leave."

Of course. He had paid on the wager. He owed her nothing more.

She moved around him toward the door, but he grasped her hand and stayed her.

"Ye've got me so I dinna ken what's up or down."

"Then the sentiment is mutual."

She disengaged from his grasp and left the hothouse. As she walked rapidly along the path toward the picnic blankets, willing away the heat in her cheeks and the quivering in her blood and the sudden acute disappointment of having gotten what she wanted but not at all what she began to realize she needed, she noticed a small carriage alongside the others.

She recognized it, as well as the soberly clad gentleman disembarking from it. Like the devil, the Reverend Elijah Waldon had arrived at the ideal moment to cause the most damage.

Her vicar was a starched, priggish pole of a Sassenach, and Duncan took a quick disliking to any parents who would seek to ally their vibrant, passionate daughter with such a man.

She affected the introductions with grace. Only a hint of dismay in her lily pad eyes conveyed her displeasure over welcoming Waldon to her party. Duncan shook the man's hand and found his grip surprisingly firm.

"How fortunate you gentlemen are," Waldon said expansively, "to enjoy the company of so many lovely ladies." He chuckled as though he'd uttered a witticism.

"Will ye join us for refreshments, Reverend?" Elspeth said.

"I should like that, my lady." With amiable, self-satisfied smiles he arranged himself stiffly on the blanket. Duncan moved to Finch-Freeworth standing apart.

"Yer sister says yer parents intend her match wi' Waldon,"

he said easily, as though the notion of it didn't clamp his stomach in a vise.

Finch-Freeworth nodded. "Is it any wonder she felt she had to do this"—he gestured to the picnic—"to escape that fate?"

Clearly her brother didn't know the entire truth of it. She was not only escaping her fate. She was trying to build a dream.

He'd done the same. Seven years ago, after he returned from the East, he'd found and killed the man that had led his sister, Miranda, to her death. Then he went to work for Myles. Every guinea he'd earned for the odd strongman jobs he'd performed had gone home to his lands. He'd made Myles pay him well and he'd sent thousands of pounds to Scotland. But putting the estate back on its feet was only part of his plan. He dreamed that someday when he died, Sorcha would inherit the estate that she so ably managed despite limitations.

That his stubborn half-sister refused to marry and produce an heir was the only weakness in that plan. If Elspeth were to inherit, it would be the end of their lands. Elspeth was as starched and prim as Waldon, and she'd give away the land management to a useless fool like their father had, and the family would be ruined once and for all.

They were nearly ruined already.

His brow loosened. All but Moira. She would live in comfort. And Lily and Abigail were finding happiness too, all because of a fiery-haired, moss-eyed whirlwind of a lady who, it seemed, was as nonplused about this all as he was.

"I saw you walk away with my sister," Finch-Freeworth said. His brow was low. "I didn't stop you because I know you've spent little time in each other's company. I think if she intends to marry you she should know who she's marrying before it's too late. But when I saw her return I regretted that I hadn't gone after you. Are you dealing with her honorably, my lord?"

"If I told *ye* I weren't, what would *ye* do?"

"I would call you out and shoot you in the heart."

"That'd put period to her plan, nou, wouldn't it?"

Finch-Freeworth's throat worked. "I care for her, Eads. She may be a curiosity to you, but she's one of the best friends of my life and here in London she's under my protection. With a word I can send her home."

"An wi' a word, sir," Duncan said quietly, "I can do the same."

Finch-Freeworth's gaze darted to Una. He swung it back. "Are you threatening me, my lord?"

"Wi' what would I threaten ye, then? The dueling pistol ye've already got pointed at ma heart?"

"With . . ." He seemed to struggle. He set his jaw. "I will not trade my sister's virtue for my happiness."

"No one's said ye must."

Finch-Freeworth's eyes were like his sister's at times, swiftly assessing, but considerably more reserved. While her emotions were on her face for Duncan to read like a book, her brother's were hidden. He'd seen the brutality of war; perhaps suffering had made him wary. Now he didn't want to believe what he was hearing.

But Duncan had noticed Una's happiness lately. He'd listened to her speak of this man with warmth and yet a guarded uncertainty that told him she was unwilling to give her heart away fully unless assured that her affections were returned. He could tell Finch-Freeworth now that the field was clear; the prize was won and he would hand it over when asked.

He didn't. A man must come to his epiphanies in his own time.

Teresa cast him a glance, saw him watching her, and smiled as though it were the most natural thing in the world.

On the other hand, a man might be dragged to his epiphany against his will.

Laughing from yet another of Mr. Smythe's thin flatteries, the moment Effie climbed from the carriage her giggling halted and her face grew weary.

"Ye dinna actually like Mr. Smythe, do ye?" Lily asked her as they ascended the hotel steps. Apparently she and Effie had burned the candle wax all night planning the wedding feast, but the betrothed twin did not seem any the worse for the lack of sleep.

Effie, on the other hand, was clearly miserable despite the day's flirtations.

"Ach," she grumbled. "Least he's no such a sissypot as Mr. Waldon."

"Sh! Dinna say such a thing." Lily darted a grin at Teresa.

"Teresa daena like that prosy old bore any more than I do. She likes Duncan. But if she marries him she'll probably start chastising me just like he does." She looked back at Teresa. "So I hope ye daena because I like ye just fine nou."

Lily laughed and squeezed her twin's hand. "Oh, Effie, I do luve ye. I wish ye could be as happy as I am."

Effie's face took on a private, fighting look. Lily released her and hurried toward the stairs to the kitchen.

Teresa went to Effie. "Perhaps it is time to try something new." When her misery and desperation had threatened to overcome her, it was what she'd done after all. The earl was right: She would not win the wager, but there was happiness to be had in her new friends' joy.

Effie screwed up her delicate nose.

Teresa led her toward the parlor. The elderly woman in black sat at the window as always. Teresa whispered, "Sometimes leaving one's own cares behind and focusing on another's can ease the unhappiness of both."

"I'm no unhappy," Effie said truculently, but she wandered into the parlor and plopped down on the piano bench. She pursed her lips then set her fingers to the ivories and tapped out a tune. It was one of her favorites, sprightly yet with an air of melancholy that made Teresa imagine Highland skies stripped with grey clouds. Effie hadn't a truly fine voice, but it was clean and sweet enough to please. When she finished, she rested her fingertips on the keys and turned to look at the old woman.

Two identical streaks of tears ran down the lady's withered cheeks. Effie's eyes went round. She went and stood awkwardly by the woman.

"Ma'am?" She fidgeted with her skirts. "I wonder if I may offer ye . . . tea?"

"Dear girl." The woman's voice was papery from disuse. "My Joseph liked me to play that song to him when he was a boy."

Effie grabbed a chair and sat on the edge of it. "What does he like to listen to nou, I wonder?"

"He wrote to me of hearing the waltz in a Vienna ballroom. He said it was magnificent."

"Weel, that must've been something, to be sure. I envy him. I've no gone anywhere, an soon I'll be back home without having seen any place but Lunnontown. But, oh, hou I'd like to travel the world!" She sighed.

"My Joseph is an officer in the Royal Navy."

"Is he yer son?"

"Grandson." Another tear chased the silvery track. "He is a fine boy. The only family I have left."

Effie chuckled. "I usually think I've far too much family." Tentatively she reached forward and gave the woman's hand a gentle pat. "Does he write to ye aften, then?"

"Every week." The skin on her aged brow was like tissue. Now it crinkled. "But I haven't heard from him in over a month. He wrote that he would come home on furlough and that I was to meet him here in London, for his time in England would be brief. I fear something dreadful has happened to him."

Effie waved a hand in the air. "Ye mustn't think like that. There's a guid explanation for it. Mebbe his horse threw a shoe, or the carriage wheel broke, or he left his luggage behind an went back for it."

"Or the tide was low in port and all the ships I could have embarked upon were grounded for weeks."

Teresa started. Beside her at the door stood a slim, broad-shouldered young gentleman in a crisp blue and white uniform, a plumed hat cocked beneath his arm.

"Joseph!" The old woman rose and teetered. Effie leaped up and grasped her arm to steady her.

"Grandmama." He came forward with a warm smile for his grandmother and Effie. The woman grabbed his arms and clung. "How good it is to see you again, my dearest," he said, lifting her gnarled fingers to his lips. "And how fetching you are in this frock." His eyes twinkled. "You haven't aged a day since we were together last Christmas." He turned his attention on Effie. "And who is this lovely lady who has so kindly kept you company in my absence?"

Effie stammered and blinked pretty eyes and said nothing. The naval lieutenant smiled and made her laugh and regarded her with warm appreciation.

Later Effie told Teresa that her heart was so full at that moment that she could not even remember her name. And by the time her sisters entered the parlor an hour later for tea, she could not in fact remember that she had ever known the world without Lieutenant Joseph P. Caruthers in it.

Chapter Nine

Calling upon her the morning after the picnic, Mr. Waldon informed Teresa that she must cut her new friends and return to Harrows Court Crossing or risk unpardonable social censure for allying herself with a family of besmirched reputation.

Apparently word had flown to Cheshire via Mrs. Biddycock's gossipy London cousin that Teresa had been seen in the company of the penniless half sisters of the scandalous Earl of Eads. Mr. Waldon insisted that the situation was unacceptable and warned that if she did not relent in her pursuit of social ruin he would inform her mother and father who were as yet ignorant of her *mésalliances*.

Teresa ignored his threats. Even if he sent a letter to Brennon Manor, her parents could not force her to return home unless they actually came to town themselves, by which time the wager would have already come to an end anyway.

Nevertheless he remained in town, insinuating himself into nearly every outing with the Eads sisters and regularly urging Teresa to return home at once. After days of resisting telling him exactly what she thought of this presumption, when he deigned to sit in judgment on the joyful announcement of Effie's betrothal to Lieutenant Caruthers, and used Lady Elspeth's disapproval of the match to support his case, Teresa exploded.

"It is insupportable," she said between gritted teeth to Sorcha and Una as they walked along the Serpentine. Lily, Moira, and Mr. Baker-Frye strolled behind them, with Lieutenant Caruthers' grandmother on Lord Eads's arm. Teresa practically felt the earl's gaze on her. She'd spent a horrid sennight longing for more caresses that he would not willingly give her. Being infatuated with a fantasy from a distance had been tortuous in its own manner. But that was nothing to being in love with a man at close range and coming to the conclusion that she should not be.

"No everybody thinks marriage is the be-all to life," Sorcha said, her steps on the path like everything she did, firm and confident. Teresa envied her attitude.

"But when the parties involved are so ideally suited"—unlike her and the Earl of Eads—"it seems criminal to discourage it." The earl did not want her and she did not now know what she wanted, but it wasn't this feeling of helplessness. "The lieutenant is an excellent person and he and Effie are besotted with each other." Their union was proceeding precisely as it should, from tea with his grandmother to walks in the park, while Teresa was foundering in confusion. "He adores her spirit and she is eager for him to haul her across the oceans to God knows where for the rest of her life. They are thrilled with each other."

"Elspeth thinks Effie'll make a poor sailor's wife," Una said, her parasol shading her cheeks from the sun.

Teresa came to a halt. "I think marriage to him will in fact be the making of her."

"Agreed," Una said. "She needs adoration, amusement, an a firm hand all at once. Lieutenant Caruthers is weel suited to give her those."

"Gird yer souls, leddies." Sorcha folded her arms. "Here come the righteous."

Ahead, Mr. Waldon and Elspeth passed Effie and Lieutenant Caruthers on the path. Lieutenant Caruthers tipped his hat, took Effie's hand securely on his arm, and drew her away. Effie's light laughter tripped behind her.

"Miss Finch-Freeworth," Mr. Waldon said as he approached. "As Lady Elspeth desires a moment's rest, may I take you on my arm now?"

She could not decline. They moved away from the group.

"I am disappointed that you have not yet returned home, Miss Finch-Freeworth," he said.

"I have not yet finished what I came to London to do," she said honestly. Lately it was not amusing to tell tales. Telling tales, after all, had gotten her here: confused and aching. It was not that the tales did not still occur to her, only that she was coming to see that they were much better confined to her stories for Freddie than spoken aloud.

Dreams were quite another thing altogether. She could never shut them away in a drawer. But they were not reality. The clergyman standing before her was reality. The future. Her future.

"I see," he said pensively. "I had hopes for you, Miss Finch-Freeworth."

She clamped down on the nausea in her stomach.

"I knew you to be lovely and well bred," he continued, "and although the childish stories with which you enjoy amusing our neighbors caused me distress and concern, I knew that in time I could mold you into an enviable wife. But now my mind and heart have taken another turn."

She released his arm but could not reply; her astonishment was too great.

"Lady Elspeth informed me of the matchmaking program upon which you have embarked," he said. "I have visited some acquaintances in town this week who assure me that this program has brought you under unflattering scrutiny in society. In my position as leader of our humble community, I must choose my wife so that she reflects upon me in the greatest light. It is with regret, therefore, that I must inform you that I have transferred my affections to a more worthy candidate, a lady of moral and social rectitude who will add to my happiness and consequence rather than subtract from them."

Teresa struggled to find her tongue. "Mr. Waldon, I wish you the very best in your newfound happiness." She refrained from shouting in joy. She was free! She would live with her parents for the rest of her life. But *she was free*!

Mr. Waldon frowned. "I had hoped for more than that."

"I assure you, I know that feeling well."

"Lily! Everybody!" Effie came skipping down the path, dragging a smiling Lieutenant Caruthers by the hand. "Joseph has asked me to marry him!"

Teresa's gaze met the earl's. She saw in his beautiful eyes that he already knew.

Four sisters betrothed. With six days left to the wager.

He knew she could not win. He liked her. He liked her

lips and he liked to touch her and he seemed to enjoy her company. That only she felt an ache in her chest when they were together and an equally fierce confusion over it was a fate she must accept.

But *must* she?

He was a lord. He needed an heir. She didn't see why she couldn't be the one to help with that.

As though he knew her thoughts, his eyes narrowed. She looked at his three un-betrothed sisters. Lady Elspeth's lips were predictably tight as the others celebrated Effie's news. And Sorcha had resisted every opportunity to meet eligible bachelors. But Una . . .

Tomorrow when she met Tobias for lunch she would finally broach the subject. She had respected his silence on the matter but she hadn't the time for playing his game now. *Her* game was about to come to an end, and she intended to win it.

Teresa was taking breakfast the following morning when the footman opened the door and Sorcha strode in.

"What a lovely surprise." She went to her. "May I offer you tea or breakfast?"

"I've come to talk," the Scotswoman said with her usual forthrightness.

Teresa's stomach did a somersault. "All right." She dismissed the footman then went to the sideboard and poured two cups of tea. "Do sit."

Sorcha's face was grim. "I dinna wish to marry, Teresa. I think ye ken it, but ye've niver asked me why."

She had avoided doing so. Knowing Sorcha's reason for

avoiding marriage might make her task more difficult, and her brother intended her to marry anyway.

Just as her parents had intended her to marry Mr. Waldon.

An obstruction seemed to lodge in her throat. She shook her head.

"I've so many ideas for our family's land. We anly lack the capital to make the improvements." Sorcha sat forward till she was on the edge of the chair. "But that's all changed nou. Mr. Baker-Frye wants to invest in ma brither's estate. He says he's always had a yearning to be a gentleman farmer, but his family's business came to him an he's got to keep it going. Moira told him aboot the troubles we've had an he's gone to talk wi' Duncan this morning."

"This is wonderful news!"

"But dinna ye see? I wish to continue as steward o' our family's lands. I've worked so hard. To be sent away nou to be housewifie to some laird . . ." She shook her head. "I canna do it."

Teresa nodded slowly, heaviness surrounding her heart. "You must tell your brother."

"I've long since told him. He willna listen. Ye've got to convince him that he mustn't force me to wed."

"He thinks I'm too meddlesome. My intervention would be more likely to hinder your case than help it." But looking into Sorcha's entreating eyes now she knew that even if the earl did not relent in his wish for his sister to wed, she must change her course. She could not be the reason that any woman did not live her dreams, even if it meant abandoning hers.

"'Tis no as ye say, Teresa. Ma brither thinks highly o' ye. He'll listen to ye if ye speak for me."

She drew a long breath. "I will try to help you."

Sorcha clasped her hand for a moment only, her grip strong and certain. "Thank ye, friend." She stood, then she paused. "But . . . I've no told ye all."

Teresa's stomach tightened. "Oh?"

"'Tis for no small purpose Duncan wishes me to wed. The Eads title an lands can descend by the female line. He wants me to inherit from him. He wants me to wed an bear sons so that ma sister Elspeth, next in line, will niver come into the land."

"But why doesn't he—"

"He'll no marry again." A crease formed between her dark brows. "I think ye care for ma brither, an it pains me to speak nou. But if he didna wed an heiress to save his lands, Teresa, he'll no wed anyone for any reason. When our sister Miranda died, then anly months later the birthing took his wifie an wee son, I think he died inside some too."

"His . . . *son?*"

"Aye. Nou do ye see?"

She nodded. Finally she saw all too clearly.

At lunch she did not encourage Tobias's confidences. If he and Una wished to fritter away their chance at happiness, she would not stand in the way of that tragedy.

She'd made an appointment with two of the brides-to-be, so to lift her spirits she dressed in her favorite walking gown, a frock of pink pinstriped muslin with tiny puff sleeves and a net fichu, and went to the hotel.

None of the Eads ladies were to be found in the parlor or their bedchambers, so she ducked into the servants' stairwell and went below. The kitchen was quiet, with only Monsieur Le Coq and Lily by stove. Lily stirred the contents of a pot in slow, wide circles.

"Guid day, Teresa!" She hefted the pan and set it on the counter. "I've been teaching Marcel hou to cook taffy. Ye've come just in time."

"Mm. Delicious." Teresa settled on a high stool and watched Lily scrape her treasure into a flat pan.

"Care for a taste, mademoiselle?" The chef snagged a thick dollop of sugared butter from the bowl and proffered it to her with a bow.

She had no heart for confections at present. But the taffy was rich and sweet and stuck to her fingers, then somehow to her cheek and brow too. She set her elbow on the counter and her chin on her palm. "So much for donning my finery for the modiste's shop."

Lily giggled. It lightened Teresa's heart. Joy could be found in little things. She would take comfort in that when this adventure was over and she was home again.

"Have you seen Moira or Abigail about?" she asked. "I was to go with them to the modiste's."

"Didna Moira's message find ye at home? The modiste hasna finished the gowns, so they all went aff to the tea room wi' Mrs. Caruthers."

"Leaving you here to cook?"

"'Tisn't a penance." She offered a twinkling smile to the Frenchman. He lifted her hand and placed a fervent kiss upon it. "They hoped ye'd join them," Lily added over her shoulder.

"Perhaps after I have another bite of this delicacy." Perhaps not at all. Perhaps she would go straight home, pack her portmanteau, and return to Harrows Court Crossing and the remainder of her life there. At least it wouldn't be spent as Mr. Waldon's wife.

That notion at least made her smile. Her smile widened as the lovebirds stared into each other's eyes.

She was seizing the moment of their distraction to lick taffy off a forefinger when Lord Eads appeared in the kitchen doorway. Her finger slid from between her lips with a pop.

A slow grin curved up one side of his mouth.

Annie had once told her that men liked to imagine things in women's mouths—for what reason, Teresa never quite discovered. So, because she would not again have the opportunity to test this, she slipped her middle finger into her mouth and sucked on it.

His grin disappeared.

"Duncan!" Lily said. "Do come taste the taffy."

He strode into the kitchen. "Forgive me for declining, but I've need o' Miss Finch-Freeworth upstairs." He grasped her hand and drew her toward the door. She tossed a shrug to Lily and the chef and allowed him to pull her into the narrow servants' stairwell.

"What is happening upst—"

He caught her mouth beneath his.

It was a hungry kiss, and she met it with all the desperate desire she felt for him but had thought she would never again be able to satisfy. Her hands found his arms then his chest. When she slipped them beneath his coat to explore the contours of muscle through his shirt she thought he would stop her. Instead a deep rumble of encouragement sounded in his chest. It set off a throbbing ache inside her. His hands cupped her behind and he dragged her against him.

She gasped and broke free of his mouth. "Are you doing this only because I licked my fingers?"

He replied with a series of kisses that grew increasingly deep and culminated in her moaning softly and struggling to press even closer to him.

"Five," he said against her cheek.

"I only licked two." He stroked the tender inner crease of her thigh and pleasure swamped her. "Clearly I should have found a batch of taffy weeks ago," she panted.

"Elspeth is five."

The import of his words penetrated her pleasure. She pushed him away with her palms.

"*Elspeth*? Are you certain?"

"Yer parents will be disappointed." The grin that lurked at the corner of his delicious mouth nearly got the best of her. Mind whirling, she fought against desire

"My parents? Whatever—" Her mouth dropped open. "Mr. Waldon!"

"Aye, Waldon." He seemed to search her face. She supposed she looked as stunned as she felt. She could not fathom it.

Then abruptly it seemed the most obvious thing in the world.

Her heartbeats lurched into a gallop.

"Five," she could only say.

He took her hand and with an inscrutable look started up the stairs. Amidst the clamor of nerves and delirious stupefaction Teresa considered telling him about the decision she had come to earlier. But she could not. She had dreamed of this—so many dreams she could not count them. Nothing could stop her now.

The door before which he halted was not in the same part of the hotel as his sisters' bedchambers. He looked down at her, a question in his gorgeous eyes.

"I'm certain," she said.

He opened the door and she stepped inside.

Sumptuous beauty was spread before her. Carpeted with cloths of rich colors, layered with giant silk cushions, and strewn with fresh pink rose petals, it looked like some sort of harem chamber. She was speechless. She had not marked him as a romantic or a seducer. But this had taken time to prepare.

"I didn't think—that is, I didn't imagine—" she stuttered. "You knew I would summon up a fifth husband?"

"Managing female," Duncan murmured, masking his satisfaction.

She turned her face up and her eyes shone with a wondering, wary light. "If you think I am so managing I wonder that you have not asked why I haven't found a willing husband for myself in all these weeks."

"Do ye?"

"Why haven't you?"

Because he was a daft fool. Because he was running as fast as he could yet losing ground. Because he needed to have her beneath him and if she belonged to another man that would never happen. Because he couldn't bear the thought of it.

He touched her cheek then slid his fingers into her silken hair. He brushed a kiss across her lips, then traced the seam with his tongue, tasting her. "A wager's a wager." She tasted of buttery sugar and she was soft everywhere—the dip beneath her ear, the contour of her throat, the curve of her neck to her shoulder. Her intoxicating lips.

She clutched him with slender hands. "You trusted that I would not renege on my part of the wager? This part?"

"Ye wanted me. No th'other way around." *Not the truth.* He had wanted her since the moment he'd seen her. He'd tried to escape to Scotland to save himself, but she hadn't allowed that.

"I did," she whispered, stretching to allow him the flavor of her neck. "I do. *Oh.*" Her hands convulsed on his shoulders. "Duncan, make love to me now before I lose my courage."

"Ye've more courage than any leddy I've ever kent, Teresa Finch-Freeworth."

"Let's not test that theory now, though. All right?"

He laughed and took her waist in his hands.

"Will you undress me?" Her voice quavered but her gaze was direct. "I understand that's preferable."

He smiled. "Aye, 'tis preferable."

"Are you teasing me?"

"No. I'm thinking hou I'm the luckiest man on earth."

Her eyelids fluttered shut. "Undress me. Please. Now. I don't think I can bear to wait another minute."

Garment by garment, slowly he revealed the body he'd been lusting over—forever, it seemed. She stood perfectly still, a rosy glow high on her cheeks and her breathing fast, and did not shy away when he finally drew the chemise over her head and discarded it.

"Yer beautiful."

Her lashes lifted. "You are still dressed."

"I've been busy."

"Remove your clothes too." She caught her plump lower lip between her teeth. "Please."

"Yer wager didna specify that."

Her eyes popped wide. "But, I—Oh. You are teasing now." Her grin was so sweet he had to taste it. She responded to his kiss with her entire naked body, wrapping her arms around his neck and pressing her lush curves to him. He filled his hands with her soft behind and made her feel his desire. She moaned. His cock jerked. He pulled her tight to him. She rocked her sex into him and slid her tongue into his mouth, and he knew that if he didn't remove her from him *now,* in a moment he'd be taking her against the bedpost still fully dressed.

That was no way for a lady to lose her innocence. *His* lady.

He peeled her off him and had to force his attention up from her spectacular breasts. The aureoles were large and dusky pink and tight with her arousal.

"Lie down," he said roughly, grabbing at one of his boots.

She pivoted to look about the chamber, her breasts swaying. "Anywhere?"

He tore at his cravat. "Anywhere."

She disposed herself on her stomach on a pile of pillows on the floor. She sank into the cushions and cast a delighted grin over her shoulder.

He couldn't unbutton his waistcoat fast enough.

She scooped a handful of rose petals and scattered them. "This is positively decadent," she purred.

"Ye've got perfect hips." He dragged his shirt over his head. "Wide. Strong. Beautiful."

"I cannot believe you are looking at my bared behind and telling me I have wide hips. I may die of shame."

"Ye've no shame to speak o'."

"It's true. I've never seen any use for it. But perhaps I should have."

He knelt and curved a palm over her buttock. She was soft. So soft. He dipped his thumb between her thighs. "I like ye shameless."

"Oh—*oh*."

"Spread yer knees, luve."

She did as commanded and he drew her back against him.

Her breaths came brokenly. "What are you doing?"

"What I've been wanting to do since I first saw ye." With his hands he guided her, stroking her against his erection until she released a long sigh. Then he nestled his cock between her buttocks.

He closed his eyes and struggled for breath.

She had stiffened. He ran his palms over her hips then her slender waist and cradled her magnificent breasts in his hands. Her breathing deepened. Giving her what they both wanted, finally Duncan released the past.

Teresa had heard that some women with large breasts could not feel acute sensation in them. She discovered now that she was most definitely not one of those women. Duncan teased her nipples into taut peaks and she felt it in her toes and lips and everywhere in between.

"Does this please ye?"

"*Yes*." She moaned and trembled and pushed back against

him. She wanted something else. Something more. She ached for it.

"Beautiful woman." He thrust against her, and again, and the rhythm of her hips swaying forward grew heavy inside her, hot and damp. She went onto her elbows, wanting and wanting, rocking and hearing his sounds of pleasure that made her wild.

"Please," she whispered. "*Please*."

His hand delved between her thighs.

Pleasure. Ecstasy. His touch was perfect. She threw her head back and moaned. "Oh, Duncan." Her body was tightening, coiling, burning with pleasure. It had never felt like this with her own hand, never—ever—

Pleasure seized her, cascading upon a series of choking moans. He turned her onto her back deep in the cushions, spread her knees, and put his hard, hot cockhead at her entrance. Then he took her virginity.

He was gentle at first, and then not so gentle because she wanted it. He was everything she had fantasized. He gave and gave, and when a droplet of sweat trickled down his chest she reached between them and gave back to him.

He groaned and thrust harder. Then harder yet. He used her deeply, completely and she clutched the cushions and convulsed again with astonished whimpers. His release was sudden and fierce.

She twined her arms around his shoulders. Still inside her, he kissed her with great tenderness, his hand stealing over her waist and stroking the swell of her hip.

Finally he rolled onto his back.

With a great sigh of satisfaction, she threw out her arms to either side. "That was very . . . *nice*."

He chuckled. "Nice, hm?"

She grinned like a cat at the cream pot—a sleepy cat lying in the sun after lapping up the entire contents of the cream pot. Her eyelids drooped.

When she awoke it was dusk and Duncan was not in the bedchamber. She had not expected him to be.

She dressed, arranged her hair, and went home.

Chapter Ten

At ten o'clock the following morning she was at the writing desk in Diantha's parlor, putting the final touches on her latest story, when Una and Tobias entered. They wasted no time in telling her their news. But she knew it before they spoke; their faces showed their joy.

"I am beside myself with happiness." She embraced Una. "It has been my dearest wish for weeks, though I didn't know if you had the courage to admit it, brother."

"Courage wasn't so much the problem."

"He thought that because he didna have a title, I was too far above him." Una's eyes crinkled. "But I set him straight."

"After your brother did." He took her hand.

"When did you ask for his approval, Toby?" Teresa tried to sound casual, as though she hadn't been wondering every second what Duncan had been doing since the moment he left her napping in his harem room.

"An hour ago," Tobias said. "He'd given it to me days ago, though. Seems he knew."

He knew. As he undoubtedly knew she loved him.

When they departed she went to her room, instructed Annie to pack her luggage, and asked the footman to inquire at the nearest posting house as to the next mail coach leaving for Manchester. She changed into her second prettiest gown—second to the gown the Earl of Eads had removed from her the day before—and walked to the hotel.

Duncan stood in the foyer with a dark, dashingly handsome man with brilliant blue eyes and an air of purpose about him.

Forcing confidence in her step, she went toward them. "My lord, I should like to speak with you."

"First allou me to make ye acquainted wi' Mr. Derek Knightly, editor o' *The London Weekly*. Knightly, this is Miss Finch-Freeworth."

"*The London Weekly*? That wonderful paper with all the splendid stories?"

"The very one," Mr. Knightly said with a quick grin. He bowed. "It's a pleasure to finally make the acquaintance of the author of quite a few splendid stories herself."

She frowned. "Me?"

"If the pages Lord Eads gave me to read are by your hand," he said with a questioning glance at the earl.

"Aye, they are." His attention was steady upon her.

"You took my stories and gave them to a newspaper editor? Without my permission?"

"I'm glad he did," Knightly said. "Your prose is genius, Miss Finch-Freeworth. Innocent panache crossed with worldly wisdom. I think the readers of *The Weekly* will love it. So I'd like to give you a regular column called 'Harpers Crest Cove Days.' How do you like it?"

"A column in *The London Weekly?*" she uttered dumbly.

"For payment, of course. As I understand you don't live in London, I'll be glad to receive your pieces via the post."

Here was her future—not what she had dreaded, nor what she had dreamed, but a fine future indeed.

"I accept, Mr. Knightly."

He smiled. "Excellent. If you'll visit me at the office tomorrow we can discuss details, including your compensation, and then I'll have my man of business see to the details."

She nodded.

"Thank you, Eads," Mr. Knightly said. They shook hands. "Until tomorrow, then, Miss Finch-Freeworth." He bowed and strode out.

She met the earl's regard. "Thank you, my lord. I should be ringing a peal over your head for taking this liberty." Her cheeks warmed. The day before he had taken much greater liberties with her after all. "But I am grateful."

"Guid."

"Now I should like to speak with you in private." She went into the empty parlor, drew in a deep breath, and turned to face him. "Though four days remain on our wager, I am hereby canceling it."

His brows bent. She wanted to surround his gorgeously square jaw with her hands, go onto her tiptoes, and kiss him until she couldn't breathe.

"Are ye?"

"I am."

Sorcha had always been honest with him, and Teresa now saw the value in telling the truth. If she'd been honest with herself she would have known that forcing a man to wed her without having his love would not give her what she wanted. She wanted love. She wanted to be swept off her feet, not to do the sweeping. She wanted a friend and lover and she thought he could be that, but not if he could not give her his heart.

Still, he didn't really need to know all of that. "I don't wish to marry you any longer. You've made me work far too hard and you are far too much trouble and I deserve better than that. But even if that weren't the case, I haven't fulfilled my part of the wager. Your sisters would have found their beaux even if I had not intervened. Except of course for Mr. Waldon. And my brother, who is infinitely happy now, so at least some good has come out of my meddling."

Sharp misery was growing in her chest. She continued before he could respond.

"Thank you for what you did for me with the newspaper." She screwed up every mote of the courage he said he admired. "And thank you for yesterday. I had a wonderful time and I hope you did too."

A muscle flexed in his jaw. "Aye, I did."

She didn't know where to set her gaze. Looking into his eyes was too painful. She went to the door. "Would you tell your sisters that I dropped by?" She would miss them dreadfully. But she would see Una now and then, and that would be a consolation.

"Teresa—"

"I have made my decision." She paused in the doorframe, her head down. "Goodbye, my lord."

He did not come after her. Nor did he call on her that evening. All along he'd wanted her to go away and she'd finally given him his wish.

The next day after Teresa visited Mr. Knightly at *The London Weekly*'s office, Diantha insisted she take their traveling carriage home to Brennon Manor. Teresa accepted. It was more comfortable to be in the company of only one's maid when tears occasionally escaped one's eyes.

Annie launched into a tale of her latest conquest: the strapping stable hand at the hotel. Teresa gave her only half an ear. Her tastes in stories, she supposed, had changed.

Duncan felt like he'd been run over by a carriage and six. Two days had passed, yet he was still as bemused as the moment she'd broken the heart he'd vowed he would never again lose. He tried to meditate and saw only her troubled eyes before him. He took a hard ride and saw only her sparkling smile. One moment he turned his horse to the north, vowing to have her even if she refused him, and the next he reined in and cursed himself for a fool.

He'd thought she wanted him. She'd given him her body. He never would have taken it if he hadn't intended to marry her. He'd been walking out the door to go tell her that when Finch-Freeworth arrived, then Knightly on his heels.

But she was a lusty female. She wanted pleasure and she'd gotten it from him. That he'd thought she wanted more only made him a common daftie.

When he'd lost Miranda, then Marie and the babe, he'd thought he could never again feel that pain. Apparently he could, all from losing a soft, strong, sweet, lush-lipped, vibrant, caring, meddlesome Englishwoman who after seven long, dark years had made him feel again.

Sorcha found him packing his traveling case. She set her fists on her hips. "What're ye doing?"

"Taking ye home where yer needed. Can ye be ready to leave come morn?"

Her eyes widened. "Did Teresa convince ye, then?"

"Convince me?"

"That ye mustn't force me to marry, o' course."

He turned fully to her, his heartbeats suddenly hard. "Sorcha, did ye understand the terms o' the wager?"

"Aye. But Duncan, I didna see hou ye could deceive her so. Ye've said for years ye'll niver marry again."

"Did ye tell her that?"

"Aye." Her forthright gaze bored into him. "It was high time somebody did."

Harrows Court Crossing was the same as Teresa had left it. Mrs. Biddycock's parlor boasted the same company—except Mr. Waldon, who was still in town—and conversation was the same old gossip.

It required less than half an hour for her to realize that the upright Reverend Elijah Waldon had lied. Mrs. Biddycock's cousin had not written from London about her. He had apparently traveled there expressly out of impatience to return her to their cozy fold. Nobody knew of her concourse with the Eads clan or anything about what she had been doing in town.

So she told them. If honesty were to be her new policy she must begin immediately.

No one believed her.

"Six matches for six Scottish ladies in three short weeks!" Mrs. Biddycock clapped her hands in delight. "I've never heard the like! Oh, Miss Finch-Freeworth, how we've missed your tales."

"My favorite part is your proposal of marriage to the penniless earl," one of the other ladies chortled. "Do tell us that part again, dear, but this time make him a duke. I simply adore dukes." She laughed merrily. Others joined in.

"But he was an earl. *Is* an earl," Teresa insisted. "And I did make a wager with him. I am telling you the truth."

"Miss Finch-Freeworth, you are priceless," another lady giggled.

Teresa left. In a muddle she walked down the high street and almost passed the big roan stallion tied before the blacksmith's shop without noticing it.

She halted, her heart careening, and stared at the horse.

The door of the blacksmith's opened and the Earl of Eads walked out. He came directly to her. She hadn't time even to untie her tongue before he went to his knee in the dusty street and placed his palm across the drape of plaid over his heart.

"Miss Teresa Finch-Freeworth o' Brennon Manor." His voice was deep and musical. "Would ye do me the honor o' marrying me?"

She blinked. "Has Sorcha gotten *betrothed?*"

The neat whisker shadow around his mouth creased into a smile and he shook his head. "Teresa, luve, say ye'll marry me."

"I told you, I—"

"I luve ye, woman. Nou promise me yer hand an make an honest man o' me." His blue eyes pleaded. "I beg o' ye."

She stepped forward, he came to his feet, and she placed her hand on his chest.

"You are real," she said stupidly. "You are not an invention of my overly active imagination. And you've just asked me to marry you. I did not fantasize it." The butterflies were doing cartwheels in her stomach, accompanied now by waltzing sparrows around the region of her heart. She shook her head. "Sorcha said you would never marry again."

"Sorcha didna have the whole story." With a smile he enclosed her hand in both of his and drew it to his lips. He kissed her knuckles, then her wrist. "I need ye, Teresa. Ye make me laugh when I've no laughed in years. Ye march to the beat o' yer own drum an I canna get enough o' ye. I want ye wi' me day an nicht. I'm determined to have ye."

Before she realized what he was about, he cinched her around the waist and knees and swept her up into his arms.

"My lord! What are you doing?" She wrapped her arms around his neck. "Put me down this instant."

"I'll make a deal wi' ye, luve. Ye promise to wed me an I'll put ye down. But keep me waiting an I'll kiss ye here."

"Hm. Which to choose? They're both tempting." She threaded her fingers through his hair. "Perhaps—"

He kissed her. She melted into him.

"Teresa," he said deeply. "Give me yer hand."

"Why didn't you say this in London?"

He let her feet slide to the ground and took her hands in his. "Ye told me ye wouldna have me," he said soberly.

"You *believed* me?"

"I did, till Sorcha told me ye'd spoken. Didna ye believe yerself?"

"Yes. But I didn't want to. Do you really love me?"

"Aye. I canna live without ye." He cupped his hands around her face and kissed her tenderly, earnestly. "Dinna make me live without ye, luve."

She threw her arms around him and he wrapped her in his embrace.

There were more kisses then, of the passionate and celebratory sort. The ladies watching avidly from the parlor window in the house across the street did not seem to mind. One or two might have even thought how wonderful it was for Teresa that she had finally found an activity that seemed to please her even more than telling tales.

Author's Note

To my wonderful readers who asked for Duncan's story, I do hope you enjoyed it.

To my new readers, it's lovely to have you along for the fun! Duncan and Teresa's first encounter at Lady Beaufetheringstone's ball takes place in my novel *How a Lady Weds a Rogue,* starring Teresa's friend Diantha and her handsome Welshman, Wyn Yale. Both Teresa and Duncan play key parts in that story. You can find the first chapters of *How a Lady Weds a Rogue* and information about all my books on my website: www.KatharineAshe.com.

Copious thank yous for assistance go to Georgie Brophy, Mary Brophy Marcus, and Marquita Valentine, without whom this story would not have come together.

I offer very special thanks to Maya Rodale for her permission to feature in this story a cameo of Regency London's most dashing newspaper editor. Mr. Knightly is a central character in her fabulous Writing Girl Series, which includes his story, *Seducing Mr. Knightly.*

Keep reading for a sneak peek at

I MARRIED THE DUKE,

the first book in the enchanting new series

THE PRINCE CATCHERS

by

KATHARINE ASHE

Available from Avon Books
September 2013

An Excerpt from

I MARRIED THE DUKE

Prologue

The Orphans

A Fair Somewhere in Cornwall
April 1804

Three young sisters of no rank and even less fortune sat in the glow of lamplight before a table draped in black velvet.

Upon that table was a ring fit for Prince Charming.

Veiled in ebony, the soothsayer studied not her clients' palms or brows or even their eyes, but the ring, a glimmering spot of gold and ruby amidst the shadows of everything else in the tent.

"You are motherless." The Gypsy's voice was rich but as English as the girls'.

"We are orphans." Arabella, the middle sister, leaned forward, tucking a lock of spun copper behind an ear formed as delicate as a seashell. Only twelve years old and already she was a beauty—lips pink as berries, cheeks blooming, eyes sparkling. In appearance she was a maiden of fairy tales, and just as winsome of temper, though any storyteller would be obliged to admit that she was not in the least bit meek.

"Everybody in the village knows we are motherless." Her elder sister Eleanor's brow creased beneath a golden braid tucked snugly into a knot. Bookish as she was, Eleanor's brow often creased.

"Our ship wrecked, and Papa adopted us from the foundling home so that we would not be sent to the workhouse." With the simple candor of the young, Ravenna explained the history she did not remember yet had often been told. She was but eight, after all. Restlessly, she shifted her behind on the soft rug, and the fabric of her skirts tangled beneath her slippers. A tiny black canine face peeked out from the muslin folds.

Arabella leaned forward. "Why do you stare at the ring, Grandmother? What does it tell you?"

"She is not our grandmother," Ravenna whispered quite loudly to Eleanor, her dark ringlets bouncing. "We don't know who our grandmother is. We don't even know who our real mama and papa are."

"It is a title of respect," Eleanor whispered back, but her eyes were troubled as she looked between Arabella and the fortune-teller.

"This ring is the key to your destinies," the woman said, passing her hand over the table, her lashes closing.

Eleanor's brow scrunched tighter.

Arabella sat forward eagerly. "The key to our true identity? Does it belong to our real father?"

The Gypsy woman swayed from side to side, gently, like barley stalks in a light breeze. Arabella waited with some impatience. She had in fact waited for this answer for nine years. Each additional moment seemed a punishment.

From without, the sounds of the fair came through the tent walls—music, song, laughter, the calls of food sellers, whinnies of horses at the trading corral, bleats of goats for sale. The fair had passed through this remote corner of Cornwall every year since forever, when the Gypsies came to spend the warm seasons on the flank of the local squire's land not far from the village. Until now, the sisters had never sought a fortune. The reverend always warned against it. A scholar and a churchman, he told them such things were superstition and must not be encouraged. But he gave freely of his charity to the travelers. He was poor, he said, but what little a man had, God demanded that he share with those in even greater need—like the three girls he had saved from destitution five years earlier.

"Will the ring tell us who we truly are?" Arabella asked.

The soothsayer's face was harsh and stunning at once, pockmarked across her cheeks but regal in the height of her brow and handsome in its strong nose and dark eyes.

"This ring . . ." the Gypsy intoned, "belongs to a prince."

"A prince!" Ravenna gaped.

"A prince?" Eleanor frowned.

"Our . . . father?" Arabella held her breath.

The bracelets on the woman's wrist jingled as she ticked a finger from side to side. "The rightful master of this ring," she said soberly, "is not of your blood."

Arabella's shoulders drooped, but her dainty chin ticked up. "Mama gave it to Eleanor to keep before she put us aboard ship to England. If it belongs to a prince, why did Mama have it? She was not a princess." Far from it, if the reverend's suspicions were correct.

The fortune-teller's lashes dipped again. "I do not speak of the past, child, but of the future."

Eleanor cast Arabella an exasperated glance.

Arabella ignored it and chewed the inside of her lip. "Then what does this prince have to do with us?"

"One of you . . ." The woman's voice faded away, her hand spreading wide above the ring again, fingers splayed. Her black eyes snapped open. "One of you will wed this prince. Upon this wedding, the secret of your past will be revealed."

"One of *us* will wed a *prince?*" Eleanor said in patent disbelief.

Arabella gripped her sister's hand to still her. The fortune-teller was a master at timing and drama; Arabella could see that. But her words were too wonderful.

"Who is he? Who is this prince, Grandmother?"

The woman's hand slipped away from the ring, leaving it gleaming in the pale light. "That is for you to discover."

Warmth crept into Arabella's throat, prickling it. It was not tears, which never came easily to her, but certainty. She knew the fortune-teller spoke truth.

Eleanor stood up. "Come, Ravenna." She cast a sideways glance at the Gypsy woman. "Papa is waiting for us at home."

Ravenna grabbed up her puppy and went with Eleanor through the tent flap.

Arabella reached into her pocket and placed three pennies on the table beside the ring, everything she had saved.

The woman lifted suddenly wary eyes. "Keep your coins, child. I want none of them."

"But—"

The Gypsy grabbed her wrist. "Who knows of this ring?"

"No one. Our mama and our nanny knew, but we never saw Mama again, and Nanny drowned when the ship sank. We hid the ring."

"It must remain so." Her fingers pinched Arabella's. "No man must know of this ring, save the prince."

"Our prince?" Arabella trembled a bit.

The Gypsy nodded. She released Arabella's hand and watched as she picked up the ring and coins and tucked them into a pocket.

"Thank you," Arabella said.

The soothsayer nodded and gestured her from the tent.

Arabella drew aside the flap, but the discomfort would not leave her and she looked over her shoulder. The Gypsy's face was gray now, her skin slack. A wild gleam lit her eyes.

"Madam—"

"Go, child," she said harshly, and drew down her veil. "Go find your prince."

Arabella met her sisters by the great oak aside the horse corrals around which the fair had gathered for more than a century. Eleanor stood slim and golden-pale in the bright glorious light of spring. Sitting in the grass, Ravenna cuddled the puppy in her lap like other girls cuddled dolls. Behind Arabella the music of fiddle and horns curled through the warm air, and before her the calls of the horse traders making deals mingled with the scents of animals and dust.

"I believe her."

"I knew you would." Eleanor expelled a hard breath. "You want to believe her, Bella."

"I do."

Eleanor would never understand. The reverend admired her quick mind and her love of books. But the Gypsy woman had not lied. "My wish to believe her does not make our fortune untrue."

"It is superstition."

"You are only saying that because the reverend does."

"I for one think it is splendid that we shall all be princesses." Ravenna twirled the pup's tail with a finger.

"Not all of us," Arabella said. "Only the one of us who marries a prince."

"Papa will not believe it."

Arabella grasped her sister's hand again. "We must not tell him, Ellie. He would not understand."

"I should say not." But Eleanor's eyes were gentle and her hand was cozy in Arabella's. Even in skepticism she could not be harsh. At the foundling home when every misstep had won Arabella a caning—or worse—she had prayed nightly for a wise, contemplative temperament like her elder sister's. Her prayers were never answered.

"We will not tell the reverend," Arabella said. "Ravenna, do you understand?"

"Of course. I'm not a nincompoop. Papa would not approve of one of us becoming a princess. He *likes* being poor. He thinks it brings us closer to God." The puppy leaped out of her lap and scampered toward the horse corral. She jumped up and ran after it.

"I do wish we could speak to Papa about it," Eleanor said. "He is the wisest man in Cornwall."

"The fortune-teller said we must not."

"The fortune-teller is a Gypsy."

"You say that as though the reverend is not himself a great friend to Gypsies."

"He is a good man, or he would not have taken in three girls despite his poverty."

But Eleanor knew as well as Arabella why he had. Only three months before he discovered them starving in the foundling home, and Eleanor about to be sent off to the workhouse, fever had taken his wife and twin daughters from him. He had needed them to heal his heart as much as they needed him.

"We shan't have to fret about poverty for long, Ellie." Arabella plucked the ring out of her pocket and it caught the midday sunshine like fire. "I know what must be done. In five years, when I am seventeen—"

"Tali!" Ravenna's face lit into a smile. A boy stood at the edge of the horse corral, shadowy, in plain, well-worn clothes.

Eleanor stiffened.

Arabella whispered, "No one must ever see it but the prince," and dropped the ring into her pocket.

Ravenna scooped up the puppy and bounded to the boy as he loped forward. His tawny skin shone warm in the sunlight filtering through the branches of the huge oak. No more than fourteen, he was all limbs and lanky height and underfed cheeks, but his eyes were like pitch and they held a wariness far greater than youth should allow.

"Hullo, little mite." He tweaked Ravenna's braid, but beneath a thatch of unruly black hair falling across his brow he shot a sideways glance at her eldest sister.

Eleanor crossed her arms and became noticeably interested in the treetops.

The boy scowled.

"Look, Tali." Ravenna shoved the puppy beneath his chin. "Papa gave him to me for my birthday."

The boy scratched the little creature behind a floppy ear. "What'll you call him?"

"Beast, perhaps?" Eleanor mumbled. "Oh, but that name is already claimed here."

The boy's hand dropped and his square shoulders went rigid. "Reverend sent me to fetch you home for supper." Without another word he turned about and walked toward the horse corral.

Eleanor's gaze followed him reluctantly, her brow pinched. "He looks like he does not eat."

"Perhaps he hasn't enough food. He has no mama or papa," Ravenna said.

"Whoever Taliesin's mama and papa were, they must have been very handsome," Arabella said, fingering her hair. She remembered little of their mother except her hair, the same golden-red as Arabella's, her soft, tight embrace, and her scent of cane sugar and rum. Eleanor remembered little more, and only a hazy image of their father—tall, golden-haired, and wearing a uniform.

The fortune-teller had not told her everything, Arabella was certain. Out there was a man who had no idea his three daughters were still alive. A man who could tell them why the mother of his children had sent them away.

The answer was hidden with a prince.

Arabella's teeth worried the inside of her lip but her eyes flashed with purpose. "One of us will wed a prince someday. It must be so."

"Eleanor should marry him because she is the eldest." Ravenna upended the puppy and rubbed its belly. "Then you can marry Tali, Bella. He brings me frogs from the pond and I wish he were our brother."

"No," Arabella said. "Taliesin loves Eleanor—"

"He does not. He hates me and I think he is odious."

"—and I aim to marry high." Her jaw set firmly like any man's twice her age.

"A gentleman?" Ravenna said.

"Higher."

"A *duke?*"

"A duke is insufficient." She drew the ring from her pocket anew, its weight making a dent in her palm. "I will marry a prince. I will take us home."

Chapter One

The Pirate

Plymouth
August 1817

Lucien Westfall, former commander of the HMS *Victory*, Comte de Rallis, and heir to the Duchy of Lycombe, sat in the corner of the tavern because long ago he had learned that with a corner at his back he could detect danger approaching from any direction. Now the corner provided the additional benefit of a limited landscape to study.

On this occasion the landscape especially intrigued.

"Ye've got the air o' a hawk about ye, lad." Gavin Stewart, ship's physician and chaplain, hefted his tankard of ale. "Is she still looking at ye?"

"No. She is looking at you. Glaring, rather." Luc took up from the table the letter from his uncle's land steward, folded the pages and tucked them into his waistcoat pocket. "I think she wants you gone."

"Wants to get at ye. They all do. 'Tis the scar." Gavin

lounged back in his chair and scratched his whiskers, salty black and scant. "Wimmen like dangerous men."

"Then you are doomed to a lonely life, old friend. But you were already, I suppose."

"Hazard o' the vows," the priest chortled. "Bonnie lass?"

"Possibly." Pretty eyes, bright even across the lamp-lit tavern, and keenly assessing him. Pretty nose and pretty mouth too. "Though possibly a schoolteacher." A cloth cinched around her head covered her hair entirely, and her cloak was fastened up to her neck. Beneath it her collar was white and high. "Trussed up as tight as a virgin."

"The mither o' our Lord was a virgin, lad," Gavin admonished. Then: "An' what's the fun if a man's no' got to work for the treasure?"

Luc lifted a brow. "Those were the days, hm, Father?"

Gavin laughed aloud. "Those were the days." He was broad in the chest like his Scottish forebears, and his laughter had always been a balm to Luc. "But since when do ye be knowing a thing about schoolteachers?"

Since the age of eleven when Luc had escaped the estate where their guardian kept him and his younger brother and blundered onto the grounds of a finishing school for gentlewomen. With a soft reprimand, the headmistress had returned him home to a punishment he could not have invented in his worst nightmares.

Luc had not believed his guardian's rants about the evils of temptation found in female flesh. Of course, he hadn't believed anything the Reverend Absalom Fletcher said after the first few months. Bad men often lied. So he escaped the following day and ran to the school, hoping to find the headmistress out walking again, and again the following day, and again, seeking an ally. Or merely a haven. Each time the footmen dragged him back to his guardian's house, his punishment for the disobedience was more severe.

He had borne it all with silent tears of defiance upon his cheeks. Until Absalom discovered his true weakness. Then Luc stopped disobeying. Then he became the model ward.

"I know about women," Luc grumbled. "And that one is trouble." He took a swallow of whiskey. It burned, and he liked that it burned. Every time she looked at him he got an awfully bad feeling.

Her movements were both confident and compact as she surveyed the crowded dockside tavern with an upward tilt of her chin as though she were the queen and this a royal inspection. Clearly she did not belong here.

Gavin set his empty tankard on the table. "I'll be leaving ye to the leddy's pleasure." He dragged his weathered body from the chair. Not a day over fifty, the Scot was weary of the sea that he had taken to for Luc's sake eleven years earlier. "Don't suppose ye'll be wanting to have a wee bit o' holiday at that castle o' yours after we leave the crew off at Saint-Nazaire? Visit yer rascally brother?"

"No time. The grain won't ship itself to Portugal." Luc tried to shrug it off, but Gavin understood. The famine of the previous year was lingering. People were starving. They could not halt their work for a holiday.

And, quite simply, he needed to be at sea.

"Grain. Aye," Gavin only said, and made his way out of the tavern.

Luc swallowed the remainder of his whiskey and waited. He did know women, of all varieties, and this one wasn't even trying to feign disinterest.

She wove her way through the rowdy crowd, taking care nevertheless to touch no one in her approach. Only when she stood before him on the other side of the table could he make out her eyes—blue, bright, and wary. The hand clutching the cloak close over her bosom was slender, but the veins beneath the pale skin were strong.

"You are the man they call the Pirate." It was not a question. *Of course it wasn't.*

"Am I?"

A single winged brow tilted upward. "They said that I was to look for the dark-haired man with a scar cutting across his eye on the right, a black-banded kerchief, and a green left eye. As you are sitting in shadow, the color of your eye is not clear to me. But you bear a scar and you cover your right eye."

"Perhaps I am not the only man in Plymouth that answers to such a description."

Now both brows rose. The slope of her nose was pristine, her skin without blemish and glowing in the fading sunlight slanting through the window at Luc's back. "There aren't any pirates now," she said, "only poor sailors with peg legs and patched up faces from the war. It is very silly and probably disrespectful of you to call yourself that."

"I don't call myself much of anything at all." Not Captain Westfall, and not the Duke of Lycombe's heir. The latter was an unstable business in any case. Luc's aunt, the young duchess, had never carried an infant past birth, despite five attempts. But that did not mean her sixth could not now survive. So in the year since he had left the navy to pursue another noble goal, he'd gone only by Captain Andrew of the merchant brigantine *Retribution*. Simple and without any familial complications, it served his purposes.

The Pirate was a foolish nickname his crew had given him.

"Then what is your real name, sir?" she asked.

"Andrew."

"How do you do, Captain Andrew?" He nearly expected her to curtsy. She did not. Instead she extended her hand to shake. She wore no ring. Not a war widow, then—the war that for years had kept his brother, Christos, safely hidden in France beyond their family's reach.

He did not take her hand.

"What do you want of me, miss, other than to lecture me on the evils of war, it seems?"

"Your manners are deplorable. Perhaps you are a pirate after all." She seemed to consider this seriously, chewing on the inside of her lower lip. The plump lip was precisely the color of raspberries.

Tastable.

Luc had not tasted a pair of sweet lips like that in far too long.

"I suppose you are an expert on manners, then?" he said with credible disinterest.

"I am, actually. But that is neither here nor there. I need passage to the port of Saint-Nazaire in France and I have been told that you depart for that port tomorrow. And that . . ." She studied him slowly, from his face to his shoulders and chest, and soft color crept into her cheeks. "I have been told that you are the most suitable shipmaster to transport a gentlewoman."

"Have you? By whom?"

"Everyone. The harbormaster, the man in the shop across the street, the barman at this establishment." Her eyes narrowed. "You are not a smuggler, are you? I understand they are still popular in some ports even since the war ended."

"Not this port." Not lately. "Do you believe the harbormaster, shopkeep, and yonder barman?"

Her brows dipped. "I did." A pause, then she seemed to set her narrow shoulders. "Will you take me to Saint-Nazaire?"

"No."

Her jaw took on that determined little tilt that made Luc's chest feel a bit odd.

"Is it because I am a woman and you will not allow women aboard your vessel? I have heard that of pirates."

"Madam, I am not—"

"If you are not a pirate, why do you cover your eye in that piratical manner? Is it an affectation to frighten off helpless women, or could you only find black cloth of that width and length?"

Clever-tongued witch. She could not possibly be teasing him. Or flirting. Not this prim little schoolteacher.

"As I believe the scar makes clear, it is not an affectation, Miss . . .?"

"Caulfield. Of London. I was recently in the personal service of a lady and gentleman of considerable status." Her gaze flittered down his chest again. "Whom I don't suppose you would know, actually. In any case, they employed me as a finishing governess for their daughter who is—"

"A 'finishing' governess?"

"It is the height of ill breeding to interrupt a lady, Captain Andrew."

"I believe you."

"What?"

"That you are a governess."

Her eyes flashed—magnificent, wide, expressive eyes the color of wild cornflowers flooded with sunlight.

"A finishing governess," she said, "teaches a young lady of quality the proper manners and social mores for entering society and leads her through that process during her first season in town until she is established. But I don't suppose you would know anything about manners or mores. Would you, captain?"

Oh. *No.* Magnificent eyes notwithstanding, he needed a sharp-tongued virginal schoolmistress aboard his ship as much he needed a sword point in his left eye.

He climbed to his feet. "Listen, Miss Whoever-You-Are, I don't run a public transport ship."

"What sort of ship is it, then?"

"A merchant vessel."

"What cargo do you carry?"

"Grain." To people who could not afford such cargoes themselves. "Now, I haven't the time for an interrogation. I've a vessel to fit out for departure tomorrow."

With that jaunty tick of her chin, she darted around a chair and moved directly into his path. "You cannot frighten me with your scowl, Captain."

"I was not attempting to either frighten or scowl. It is this inconvenient affectation, you see." He tapped his finger to his cheek and stepped toward her.

She remained still but seemed to vibrate upon the balls of her feet now. She was a little slip of a thing, barely reaching his chin yet erect and determined.

He couldn't resist grinning. "You don't look any taller to me standing on your toes, you know. I am uncowed."

Her heels hit the floor. "Perhaps you take pleasure in playing at notoriety with this pirate costume."

"Again with the pirate accusation." He shook his head. "You see no hook on my wrist or parrot on my shoulder, do you? And I have all the notoriety I wish without pretending a part." *Heirs to dukedoms typically did,* even Luc, despite his estrangement from his uncle. But now the latest letter from the duke's steward sounded desperate; the fortunes of Combe were in jeopardy. However much he wished to help, Luc hadn't the authority to alter matters there. He was not the duke yet. Given his young aunt's interesting condition, he might never be.

He closed the space between them. "As to the other matter, I take pleasure in a man's usual amusements." He allowed himself to give her a slow perusal. She was bound up snugger than a nun, in truth. But her lips were full, and her eyes . . .

Truly magnificent. Breathtaking. Full of emotion and intelligence he had absolutely no need of in a woman.

"I daresay," she said. The magnificent cornflowers grew direct. "Name the price I must pay for you to give me passage to Saint-Nazaire and I will double it."

He scanned the cloak and collar. Pretty, yes. Gently bred, indeed. Governess to society debutantes, possibly. But now she was alone and begging his help to leave Plymouth.

Suspicious.

"You cannot pay double my price."

"Name it and I will."

He named a sum sufficient to sail her to every port along the Breton coast and back three times.

Her cheeks went slightly gray. Then the chin came up again. In the low-beamed tavern packed with scabrous seamen she looked like a slim young sapling in a swamp, and just as defiant. "I will pay it."

"Will you now?" He was enjoying this probably more than he ought. "With what, little schoolteacher?"

The cornflowers narrowed. "I told you, I am a governess, a very good one, sought after by the most influential families in London. I have sufficient funds."

With a swift movement he slipped his hand into the fold of cloak about her neck and tugged it open.

She grabbed for the fabric. "What—?"

His other hand clamped about her wrist. Her gown was gray and plain along the bodice and shoulder that he exposed, but fashioned of fine quality fabric and carefully stitched. And hidden beneath the fabric stretched over her throat was a small, round lump.

"Not a little schoolmistress, it seems," he said.

"As I have said." For the first time her voice quavered.

"You do look like a governess." Except for the spectacular eyes. "More's the pity."

Her breasts rose upon a quick breath, a soft pressure against his forearm that stirred a very male reaction in him that felt dispiritingly alien and remarkably good.

"My employers prefer me to dress modestly to depress the attentions of rapacious men," she said. "Are you one of those, Captain?" Her raspberry lips were beautifully mobile. He wanted a glimpse of the sharp tongue. If it were half as tempting as her lips, he might just take her on board after all.

"Not lately," he said. "But I'm open to inspiration."

The raspberry lips flattened. "Captain, I care nothing for what you believe of me. I only want you to allow me to hire passage on your ship."

"I don't want your gold, little governess."

"Then what payment will you accept?" She sent a frustrated breath through her nose, but her throat did a pretty little dance of nerves. *By God,* she truly was lovely. Not even her indignation could disguise the pure blue of summer blooms, dusky lashes, delicate flare of nostrils, soft swell of lips satiny as Scottish river pearls, and the porcelain curve of her throat. And her scent . . . It made him dizzy. She smelled of sweet East Indian roses and wild Provençal lavender, of Parisian four-poster beds and the comfort of a woman's bosom clad in satins and lace, all thoroughly at odds with her modest appearance and everything else in this port town.

"I can cook and clean," she said. "If you prefer labor to coin, I will work for my passage to Saint-Nazaire." Her voice grew firmer. "But my body is not for sale, Captain."

Governess and mind reader at once, it seemed.

"I don't want that," he lied. His hand slipped along the edge of the linen wrapped about her head. Her eyes were wide but she remained immobile as his fingertips brushed the satiny nape of her neck. Her hair was like silk against his skin, the bundle inside the linen heavy over his knuckles. Long. He liked long hair. It got tangled in all sorts of interesting ways when a woman was least aware of it.

"Then . . ." Her lips parted. Kissable lips. He could imagine those lips, hot and pliant, beneath his. *Upon him.* She would be hot and pliant all over. He could see it in her flashing eyes and in the quick breaths that now pulled her gown tight over her breasts. Cool and controlled she wished to appear, but that was not her true nature.

Her true nature wanted his hands on her. Otherwise she would be halfway across the tavern by now.

"What do you want?" Her words came unsteadily again.

"Aha. Not as starchy as she appears, gentlemen," he murmured beneath a burst of rough laughter from a table of sailors nearby.

"What do you know of gentlemen?"

Too little. Only those moments during the war when Christos was safely stowed at the château and Luc had been able to enjoy the company of his fellow naval officers, as the lord he had been born to be.

"An expert on the subject, are you?" His fingertips played.

"No. What do you want?" she repeated flatly.

"Perhaps this?" His thumb hooked in the ribbon about her neck. She gasped and tried to break free. He twisted the ribbon up and the pendant popped from the gown's neck.

Not a pendant. A man's ring, thick and gold with a ruby the size of a six pence that shimmered like blood.

"*No.*" She slapped her hand over the ring.

Luc released her and stepped back. Lovely, yes indeed. But she did not look like a man's mistress. She was too plainly dressed and far too slender to please any man with money to spend in bed.

But appearances could deceive. Absalom Fletcher had looked like an angel.

"What is it?" he said. "A gift from an appreciative patron?"

She seemed to recoil. "No."

"He has poor taste to give you his ring instead of purchasing a piece for a lady. You should have thrown him off much earlier. Or haven't you? Are you going to him now?"

The cornflowers shuttered. "This ring is none of your business."

"It is if you intend to carry it aboard my ship. That's no mean trinket you have there. Where are you going with it?"

She stuffed it back into her dress. "I am traveling to a house near Saint-Nazaire to take up a new position at which I must report before the first of September. And what do you think you're doing, reaching down a helpless woman's gown? You should be ashamed of yourself, Captain."

"If you are helpless, madam, then I've something yet to learn about women."

"Perhaps you should learn generosity and compassion first. Will you take me aboard?"

Beautiful face. Gently bred. Desperate for help. A rich man's cast-off mistress. Eager to leave Plymouth. Had she stolen the ring?

He didn't need this sort of trouble.

"No," he said. "Again." He headed toward the door.

A great stone seemed to press on Arabella's lungs. It could not end like this, rejected in a seedy tavern by a man who looked like a pirate, and all because she had been foolish enough to miss her ship.

But she could not have left those children alone, the little one no more than three and his brothers trying so valiantly to be brave while frightened. The eldest, dark and serious, reminded her of Taliesin years ago, the reverend's student and the closest to a brother she had ever known. She could not have abandoned the children like their mother did, even if she had known it would cause her to miss her ship.

The ship that would take her to a prince.

He would not remain at the château long. The letter of hire said the royal family would depart for their winter palace on the first of September. If she arrived after that, she must find her own way.

She always sent all her spare funds to Eleanor; she had no money to spend on more travel. And she simply must make an excellent impression. She would prepare the princess for her London season. Then perhaps—if she were very lucky and dreams came true—the prince would come to admire her. It would not be the first time one of her employers had turned his attention toward her, liking the pretty governess a bit too much. Not the first by far.

This time, however, she would welcome it.

She twisted her way through the crowded tavern in the captain's wake. His back was broad, his stride confident, and men made way for him.

"I beg you to reconsider, Captain," she called to him as he passed through the door to the street. Her fists balled, squeezing away panic. "I must reach the château before the first of September or I will lose my new position."

He halted. "Why didn't you book passage on a passenger ferry?"

"I did. I missed my ship." She chewed the inside of her lip, the only bad habit from childhood that she had not been able to quell. The public coach from London had rattled her bones into a jumbled heap. But anticipating the sea voyage proved so much worse. For two decades her nightmares had been filled with swirling waters, jagged lightning, and walls of flame. She'd been tucked in a corner of the posting inn's taproom, struggling to control her trembling, when the call for her ship's departure sounded. She had forced herself to her feet and out the door by sheer desperation to know once and for all who she really was.

Then, in the inn yard, she encountered the children.

"I had a matter of some importance to see to," she evaded.

Lamplight cast unsteady shadows across the captain's face. Probably it had been a very handsome face before the scar disfigured it, with a strong jaw shadowed now with whiskers and a single deep green eye lined with thick lashes. His dark hair caressed his collar and tumbled over the strip of cloth tied about his head.

"A matter of more importance than your new position at a *château?*"

He did not believe her.

"If you must know," she said carefully, "I have three children I must take to their father this evening before I travel to France."

He looked blankly at her. "Children."

"Yes." She turned and gestured to the curb beneath the eave of the tavern. Three little bodies huddled against the wall, their eyes fixed anxiously upon him. "Their father awaits them across the city. While I was attempting to contact him, my ship departed without me," taking with it her traveling trunk, another trouble she could not think about until she solved her first problem. But the daily cruelties of the foundling home had taught her resourcefulness, and working for spoiled debutantes had taught her endurance. She would succeed.

"I am relieved—" Captain Andrew's fingers crushed his hat brim, the sinews of his large hand pronounced. "I am relieved to learn that you take pride in your progeny even as you abandon them."

"You have mistaken it, Captain," she said above the clatter of a passing cart, making herself speak as calmly as though she were sitting in an elegant home in Grosvenor Square recommending white muslin over blush silk. "They are not my children. I encountered them only in the posting inn yard. Their mother had abandoned them, so I determined to find their father for them."

The captain turned toward her fully then, his wide shoulders limned in amber from the setting sun that lightened his hair with strands of bronze. In his tousled, intense manner, he was not commonly handsome, but harshly beautiful and strangely mythic. His dark gaze made her feel peculiar inside. *Unsolid.*

His lips parted but he said nothing, and for a moment he seemed not godly but boylike. Vulnerable.

She tilted her head and made herself smile slightly. "I can see that I have surprised you, Captain. You must reevaluate matters now, naturally. But while you are doing so I do hope you will reconsider the plausibility of me being mother to a twelve-year-old boy." She paused. "For the sake of my vanity."

He grinned, an easy tilt of one side of his mouth that rendered a pair of masculine lips devastatingly at the command of a grown man indeed.

"How callous of me." He crossed his arms and leaned his shoulder against the doorpost. "I beg your pardon, madam."

"Without any sincerity whatsoever, it seems. I pray you, sir, will you take me to Saint-Nazaire?"

The grin slid away, leaving the vibrant scar dipping over his right cheek yet more pronounced. He must have suffered the injury recently. The war had been over for a year and a half, but he bore the erect carriage and authoritative stance of a naval commander.

It wouldn't matter if he were the head of the Admiralty and his vessel a hundred-gun ship of the line, as long as he carried her swiftly to her destination.

"How did you determine the location of their father's home?" he said.

"I asked about. I can be persistent when necessary."

"I am coming to see that." He pushed away from the doorway and started off along the street. "Come."

"*Come?*" She gestured to the children and hurried after him.

He looked down at her as she awkwardly tried to match his long strides, and he halted mid-street. He did not seem to heed the traffic of horses and carts and other pedestrians, but stood perfectly solid before her like he owned the avenue. His eye glimmered unsteadily, a trick of the setting sunlight, she supposed. It was a very odd sight. He seemed at once both in thorough command and yet confused.

He pointed at a building across the street. "Give my name to the man that you find on the other side of that door and tell him that I said he is to escort you to the children's home and return you to your inn tonight."

"But—no." Arabella's cold hands were pressed into her skirts. "You needn't. That is to say—"

"He is a good man, in my employ, and you and the children will be considerably safer crossing this town with him than without." He scowled again. "You will do this, Miss Caulfield, or I will not take you to Saint-Nazaire on my ship."

Her heart turned about. "You will take me there?" Upon his ship. Upon the sea.

She must.

He scanned her face and shoulders. "To whose home are you traveling, little governess?"

He was no longer teasing. She must be honest. "I am going to Saint-Reveé-des-Beaux. It belongs to an English lord, but the Prince of Sensaire is in residence there and he has hired me to teach his sister before her debut in London society at Christmastime."

"Saint-Reveé-des-Beaux," he only said.

"Do you know it, Captain?"

"A bit." His brow cut downward. "Miss Caulfield . . ."

"Captain?"

"My ship is not a passenger vessel. There will be no other women, no fine dining or other amusements. Aboard it, you will be at my mercy. Mine alone. You do understand that, do you not?"

"I . . ." She hadn't given it thought after so many people in port recommended him. Naïvely, she had assumed it meant he was a gentleman. But gentlemen had lied to her before.

She had no choice. "I understand."

"We depart at dawn, with or without you."

He moved away, and Arabella released a shaking breath. Forcing a bright smile, she pivoted about and beckoned the children to her.

Author Bio

With the publication of her debut novel in 2010, KATHARINE ASHE earned a spot among the American Library Association's "New Stars of Historical Romance." Amazon awarded *How to Be a Proper Lady* a place among the Ten Best Books of 2012 in Romance, *When a Scot Loves a Lady* is a nominee for the 2013 Library of Virginia Literary Award in Fiction, and in 2011 Katharine won the coveted Reviewers' Choice Award for *Captured by a Rogue Lord*. Reviewers call her books "breathtaking," "lushly intense" and "sensationally intelligent."

Katharine lives in the wonderfully warm Southeast with her beloved husband, son, dog, and a garden she likes to call romantic rather than unkempt. A professor of European history, she has made her home in California, Italy, France, and the northern United States. Please visit her website at www.KatharineAshe.com.